# AND DO THE DEAD FEEL SPRING?

by

Christopher Billing

Published by New Generation Publishing in 2012

Copyright © Christopher Billing 2012

First Edition

The author asserts the moral right under the Copyright, Designs and Patents Act 1988 to be identified as the author of this work.

All Rights reserved. No part of this publication may be reproduced, stored in a retrieval system or transmitted, in any form or by any means without the prior consent of the author, nor be otherwise circulated in any form of binding or cover other than that which it is published and without a similar condition being imposed on the subsequent purchaser.

www.newgeneration-publishing.com

 New Generation **Publishing**

# INTRODUCTION

Although this book has been categorised as fiction I would have the reader know that the skeleton of the story is very much factual. Howard Hardy, the main character, was my maternal grandfather who committed suicide in November, 1936. Lois, his wife, my grandmother, died in 1979, a very private person, who never to my re-collection mentioned his name once in conversation. His daughter, Betty, my mother, was nine at the time of her father's death, and due to the social stigma of suicide, was excluded from his funeral. Not only that, but Howard's life and very existence seems to have been swept firmly under the carpet and contact with his side of the family was severed. The result being that mum has very few details pertaining to Howard. Subsequently, the main events in the story are the factual bones that I have attached my (fictional) commentary upon.

During my early years Howard would occasionally crop up in conversation. For example, mum retained a few of his possessions - his piano and a small number of wooden items that he had made, as he was a woodwork teacher as well as being the English master and the eventual headmaster of the local school. Also, I remember times when the family would pore over our photographs and mum might say something like "doesn't he (me) look like Howard".

And so, Howard had a very minor, but shadowy, part in my growing up.

However, in 1998, during my 46th year, all that changed. I was living in Tucson, Arizona at the time and was literally taken over with the desire to write about this man I'd never met. A strange synchronicity was also at play: Howard was 46 when he died. Throughout the following year I wrote three versions of my story. Eventually the story became the one you are about to read. And although I have written a lot during my lifetime, not only was I not phased by the challenge of sustaining a story of 40,000 words or so - considering the average poem I write may be 12-20 lines - I was particularly conscious of the fact that the story wrote itself: It developed very naturally, without any formal planning or structure - In short, it arrived with very little struggle. It was as if I was a conduit to relay his story.

And so, after writing such a book as this, what am I left with? Well, for one thing, many more questions:

Was it worth it?

Why would I happily donate so much time writing about a man who I never met and whose DNA is partly in me?

And the list goes on...

Is this fiction?

Who's to say it isn't?

Obviously I can't claim it to be factual. However, I return here to the ease at which I wrote the piece and the way Howard's character blossomed naturally and without conscious contrivance.

Was I writing from a shared gene pool? An interesting thought to mull over.

Coming back to Howard, I must say at this point that I don't consider him a hero. In fact, he is like millions of other young men, throughout time, who have yearned for something that seemingly remains, due to circumstances out of his control, forever out of reach: He is, and remains on the surface thwarted, and yet in many ways, rewarded.

Also, his is not a war story, although it seems that war was the source of his frustration. Neither is this a romance: Merely one of lost love and an attempt to rectify the situation.

There is also no readily identifiable theme in the story, save that of Howard's attempts to put his life back together again. If anything the story hopes to reflect the ups and downs in all our lives, regardless of circumstances, and goes a long way in questioning what success, or indeed its counterpoint, is really about.

Life is always much more than what we make of it, burdened, as we are, with its daily grind that seems to blind us to many of the silver linings that we are in search of.

And suicide, what of that?

The effects of trauma and life threatening disease on the individual are of course totally subjective. The latter will prompt Howard to his suicide. The former, however, will bring about changes in his life that before he had no thought of, and will be the subject of the sequel I am at this time writing.

As a retired counsellor and therapist of more than 20 years' experience I have witnessed the countless and varied affects that tragedy has brought to the lives of individuals. One of the most common affects is one of an insidious nature that makes the victim question everything that he once believed in, in an attempt to regain what he perceives he's lost, whilst paralleling this with what the world in general has lost.

And Do the Dead Feel Spring is an introduction into, and indeed a tribute to, not only Howard Hardy, but also the millions of 'inexperienced and naïve' young men and women who have, over the years, sacrificed both body and mind to the cause of freedom.

The few actual events of Howard's life passed down to me have been blended into a storyline using commentary, narrative, journal entries and letters of my own creation, that will, I hope, convey the overriding dilemma of the inexperienced and naive, as they are at first faced with the brutal realities of war, and then afterwards, with the seemingly endless task of coming to terms with all that they have seen, done and experienced: The eternal questioning, reasoning, qualifying and justifying; together with their lasting consequences.

I have a belief that when we no longer fear death, not only does living become more focused and less fearful, but dying itself becomes part of life's natural process. In this, Howard's suicide then becomes a level-headed response to an unchangeable circumstance: an honest acknowledgment of the fact that his race is run.

Within this spectrum is what is termed today as grief: It's symptoms; how they affect our lives; how grief provokes sobering realisations; and finally if the process is worked through diligently, there are rewards - some expected, some not.

I hope you find this book not only interesting, but also evocative enough to influence and challenge your beliefs, as it did my own.

Christopher Billing.
September, 2012.

Cover photograph of Howard's grave courtesy of Sally Knight.

# WITH THE END IN SIGHT. 1936.

In the lounge of their cottage, built snugly into the side of a valley, sat a middle-aged man. He sat, smiling proudly, in his high-backed, leather armchair. At his side stood a young girl of eight or nine. There was a celebration in progress and she was wearing a white fluffy party dress with matching socks and shoes.

"Now come on you two, keep still and smile". The voice of the photographer was growing impatient. They both smiled.

Without any warning, he heard the plaintive cry, echoing around the valley and through the partially opened window in the lounge.

"It's getting a bit chilly in here, can you close the window, Howard, please?"

Howard slowly got up and moved towards the window. He stood there looking out over the valley, smiling. There was a rainbow rapidly becoming more vivid, and the watery-bright sunlight danced in his eyes and on the lens' of his spectacles. He remained still, breathing in the fresh country air, and as his eyes briefly closed he felt young again. In and in he breathed, the freshness intoxicating. When his lungs could take no more he held the breath and as his eyes slowly opened there was peace in his body. A feeling he had not enjoyed for some time. In that moment all was well, there was no pain or fear, just a tranquil state of being. Motionless, he looked out over the valley. He knew it well; it was his valley, or so he liked to think. He had moved back there some fifteen years previously when his father became too ill to look after himself: His mother had died a year previously and then, shortly after he moved back his father had also died. From nowhere, it seemed, came a wife and then a child. He had never intended to marry, considering himself too busy at the grammar school.

Apart from his time at college in Nottingham he had lived in Melton all his life. He loved the countryside, and gradually became *part of it.* After he qualified as a teacher he had fled back there as quickly as possible, appalled at the city life, the poverty and the airless industrial death that seemed to hang there: The chimneys spewing their filth from the factories that had spread over the once green land like a cancer. His subject was English, he even wrote himself, but that was for his own pleasure.

He was also good with his hands and loved creating things for the cottage. Wood had a life and a personality of its own and he would work intently for hours, shaping, rubbing-down, staining, sanding again and polishing, extracting the very best from both form and grain. He had believed his lifestyle would go on, unaltered, until the end.

Understandably, when the notion of marriage came into his life he was torn emotionally and for Howard the tear would never really mend. He tried desperately to bring the two worlds together within himself, but they were as opposed to each other as he and his wife were turning out to be.

Lois, two years older than Howard, was the youngest of five children from a farming family in nearby Wenfield. She had been the classical 'baby' of the family and had lived a pampered life at the hands of siblings, parents and would-be suitors alike. By the time she and Howard married in 1925, she was not only a 'fine and handsome woman', but headstrong and unbridled to boot. She was used to her own ways and the shock of her new responsibilities had all but broken up their marriage during those harsh, early days. However, amidst this marriage grounded in love they had quickly developed a compromise that allowed two, bitingly independent beings to come together to share and value something quite unique. This allowed Howard to remain thoughtful and sensitive, while she continued in her need to be impulsive, out-going and to a degree, looked after. One thing they did have in common however was a love of the countryside and it was this shared enjoyment that helped keep them together until late in 1926 when she told him she was pregnant.

Lois and Howard were 38 and 36 years old respectively when the prospect of parenthood suddenly appeared. It was something that neither had seriously considered nor to any degree discussed. It was almost as if they had left it to nature to decide for them. As it was, it had the effect of turning this outwardly demure couple into excited, young lovebirds. And Howard, full in the throes of anticipated fatherhood, had jokingly pointed out that it was the first thing that they had truly collaborated in. And as the birth approached it seemed to the both of them that they had found the secret to marital harmony, however accidentally it had occurred.

DH Lawrence spoke to Howard as no-one had done before, and in the classroom he regularly spoke for him, through his novels and poetry that slowly began appearing from 1910 with the publishing of his first book, The White Peacock. Lawrence was born, not far away across the border in Nottinghamshire, five years before Howard. They had similar upbringings and witnessed the same destruction of rural England: The once green hills turning to slag-heaps as great industrial eyesores filled the landscape. And with the eyesores came the cheap back-to-back houses that clustered around the mines and the factories. Thin and mean, grey, cobbled streets led to the factory gates and mines where men, women and children in their droves worked long hours a day for a pittance. But the two had moved on, not accepting what their fathers had blindly followed. They had broken the mould and had escaped. Howard became a teacher and fled back to the countryside. Lawrence would flee the frustrations of teaching to become a wanderer writing novels that seemed to Howard to both right the wrongs and dignify the people and places of his upbringing. But there was more, much more than Howard, at first, could comprehend. Lawrence was defining a new line of thought, a new way to experience life, with all its ups and downs - a new way to love, regardless of gender a return for man to his natural state; at one with himself and the world around him. Ironically, though these men would never meet, both would share one final, dark experience: A premature death. And two, vital lives would be cut short. Two husbands and fathers, and the shock waves would send ripples through the lives of those they left behind, and those to come.

They had quickly become inseparable. In the early years, when she cried during the night, it was he who would answer the call, he who would cradle her lovingly in is arms, talk and sing quietly to her until she fell back, once more to sleep. And as she got older, it was she who accompanied him on his frequent walks through the valley and out into the hills. He had so much to share with this little life and she, for her part, soaked up all he had to give. He loved her and understood her well: she grew into the missing link in his life, maybe an underlying and unconscious reason for his marriage. His life seemed fulfilled, complete.

For her part, Lois welcomed his involvement and genuinely delighted in the two of them creating such a healthy bond. To her it seemed very natural as she harked back to her own upbringing with the copious attention she received, from her father and brothers.

Standing at the window, answering the call of the

all-knowing cry, he looked up into the heavens and smiled. And then, without reason, he waved. He saw the rainbow and waved and mouthed 'hello', over and over, as his head rolled slowly, wondering, yet all the while knowing. It was then that he coughed silently into his ready handkerchief, and as it unfolded he saw the bright red flower of death in the crumpled cotton.

He stared back out into the valley and at once became aware, as a chill ran through him, that life was surely running out for him. He shrugged and smiled wryly, and lowering his head gazed blindly into the carpet as soft, sad tears ran down his face. He knew it was over.

"Howard, Howard... what's wrong?"

"Daddy...!"

"Oh it's nothing... nothing really"

She'd seen her father cry before, but then she had sensed it was about happy things. Sometimes when he kissed her goodnight or when he met her from school. There was so much joy in his heart for her that all he seemed able to was cry. Maybe he knew, long before he'd heard the cry, that those moments, simple as they were, should be cherished and kept for a time when there would be nothing but memories. A time when he might only be able to watch and hope.

He slowly turned to his family and smiling, repeated his words. " It's all right, it's nothing." He held out his arms and they came in to him.

"Oh mother, I'm sorry..." He sobbed into her shoulder, his whole body shaking. "...There's nothing I can do now but wait."

Wait? Wait for what? What was it he wasn't telling her? And today of all days; her birthday. And what was he sorry for? For crying?

He had shared his whole life with her and in a way he had grown closer to her than his wife. There seemed to be a lot he didn't understand about himself, but he now realized how much easier it was to love a child, while recently it was becoming easier for Lois and he to retreat from each other.

With Lois he had to explain and be accountable, with Betty he was still able to be dad and not have to go into details.

The fear of the inevitable drove a wedge between Lois and Howard; a cold, fearful space and was ashamed of himself for it. He longed to reach out to her, but all he seemed capable of were smiles that he hoped would say more than words. In a way they were becoming good friends. For Lois, the more outgoing of the two, she was devastated. She couldn't, or more accurately, wouldn't, accept the facts. Safety became the order of the day and this arrangement suited them both. There were no rows, no bitterness, just an air of stifled hope. They supported each other, in and out of the house, they cared, and in a unique fashion this love for each other grew into something that Howard believed was very special: they shared a common dignity.

How he had contracted tuberculosis he wasn't sure, although his exposure to poison gas during the war seemed the obvious reason; and he had surely been consumed by it, as its previous name, consumption, suggested. Howard had been suffering, on and off, for years now, and recently he had felt its pain increase. The doctor had duly increased his medication and had suggested that Howard was entering the final furlong. The pain, the coughing and the blood were almost bearable, but what Howard found the hardest were the sad faces of his wife and daughter; helpless to do anything but watch his decline.

Teaching had become difficult and he had grudgingly become a part-timer; going in when he felt strong enough, or when he couldn't bear the isolation of resting any longer. He'd always been an active man, but life now demanded the opposite of him, and for Howard this could only mean a slow, painful and lingering death.

It was spring and he knew the deep significance of the season: his birthday was two days before his daughter's. It was a time of renewal, a time for growth and change. It was time too for sadness and the gathering of important memories that had clung to him for twenty one years now. The final line of a poem he'd written all those years before was in his head - 'As their tears fill my eyes'. He'd heard the call of spring echo around the valley. At first it had frightened him, but today he had acknowledged it and greeted it with a soft 'hello'.

# 1912

At twenty two, Howard believed his life to be all but perfect. He'd trained and earned his teaching certificate, and even done a year in the city before landing the perfect job at St Thomas's School in Melton. He'd always been eager to learn and subsequently school had become a natural second home for him. And so, when he returned to teach at the school that he had attended as a pupil, it was indeed like, coming home; though he had to concede that the old grey-stone, early Victorian buildings, were as ever, far from welcoming. But for Howard, sights as well as sounds were secondary to the overall delight he felt upon his return. The school housed just over 150 pupils, and Howard's time would be equally split between English and Woodwork, with classes comprising of students from all grades. It would be challenging and he knew he would be scrutinised by his peers, some of whom had been his guiding lights some four years previous, but it would be, on the whole, stimulating to renew the old friendships and ultimately, prove his worth. His wage was three pounds, one and sixpence a week less stoppages, a good wage for the time, and he would be once more, living at home; back in the countryside again! He had sent the majority of his luggage ahead in order that when the 9:15am from Nottingham slowed to a halt at Melton station, the mile walk home would be easily managed.

It was Saturday, April 12th, 1912 and Howard was twenty two years and two days old. The weather was cool, but dry, and he was delighted to see his parents' familiar shapes awaiting him on the platform as he leaned out of the window of the slowing, steaming train. Amidst the smoke from the engine he breathed the familiar country air. It smelt green and closing his eyes for an instant he saw the hills and the valleys, the grazing animals and the trees, washing hanging out to dry and the smell of home cooking.

Although born and raised in the country, Howard was not a hunter: he was an observer. He would hike and climb, paint when the mood took him, but mostly he would sit on 'his hill' and write. Write poems, letters and his journal. There was something so peaceful about home that made creativity second nature, surrounded as they were by open pastures and rolling hills. And when the weather was wet there was always his father's workshop, where he could create all sorts of things. There was an old shotgun that had been handed down by his grandfather, but that had now hung for as long as he could remember under an increasing blanket of rust, cobwebs and dust on the back wall of the workshop.

When the war came he knew he'd have to carry a gun and he remembered how alien it felt to have this cold object of death, primed and ready, in a holster at his side. He had been trained with both rifle and pistol, but as an officer he only had to carry the pistol. During those weeks of training he had carried the burden of his conscience. He wasn't cut out for all this, but what could he do? Wasn't he about to fight a just war for the good of mankind and remove the threat of an aggressive Germany and Austria?

Britain declared war on August $4^{th}$, 1914. He'd watched the situation grow steadily out of control during the previous weeks. At first he believed the fire could be easily doused by the most basic use of diplomacy. But as the days passed he grew in horror as he witnessed a world that wasn't interested in discussion or compromise. Rather it was turning out to be some kind of crazy free for all, with the winner taking all. By the end of July, 1914, entente was a forgotten word and about three quarters of the *civilised* world was preparing to wage war for reasons that no-one appeared particularly sure of. But it was too late to back down now. One couldn't lose face this late in the day. And when it happened there was the feeling of a line of dominos falling:

Austria/Hungary declares war on Serbia

Germany declares war on Russia

Germany invades friendly neighbour, Belgium

Britain and Belgium declare war on Germany

Austria declares war on Russia

Serbia declares war on Germany

Britain and France declare war on Austria

Japan declares war on Germany

Britain declares war on Turkey

Turkey declares war on Britain, France and Russia

Italy declares war on Turkey

Germany declares war on Portugal

Italy declares war on Germany

America declares war on Germany
By the time America joined the war in April 1917, Howard's war would be over, after first being on the western front and then in Gallipoli. And although it was

over he would forever feel that this experience would remain as a shadow over him, until he died in 1936.

# THE WALKING WOUNDED
# FEBRUARY, 1915.

"If there had've been more regulars, maybe we'd have made more sense of it, though fighting the Boers would've been little preparation for the trenches…"

Corporal Alan Blair, better known to Howard as 'Ally', had taught mathematics at Melton and had joined the staff two years before Howard, in 1910. He'd been one of the first in the area to sign up and had returned at the beginning of March with multiple shrapnel injuries. His experience of the Western Front had put years on him, while his eyes had that distant, pained look about them that spoke of the horrors they'd witnessed. He now walked with a stick.

Howard had been instrumental in organising a swift pint at the Lamb Inn, just across the road from the parish church, in order to pick Ally's brains as to what this war was actually like.

"… it would be hard for anyone or anything to prepare another for the Marne, where I was, or any other battle around that time, from Albert and Arras, Vimy and Loos to Festubert and Neuve Chapelle."

"Just exactly what do you mean Ally. The paper's say it's all going well and the German's are in check?"

"What I mean is Howard, you aren't getting accurate news back here. At best, you're getting a positive overview, nothing more."

"So what is going on then?"

"Murder, despair, horrors, madness, death. Oh yes, don't let's forget death shall we. It's crazy Howard, only back last August Rupert Brooke was writing 'Now God be thanked, who has matched us with this hour', and ever since it has been my experience that *over there*, anyway, men have been trying to understand this monstrously foolish act. And if they don't understand it, they wonder how we could've been so bloody foolish to think that something glorious could come from all this. And even when Brooke himself suggested that 'If I should die...' not even that could deter the national spirit. And it has become glorious, not only to fight, but also now, to die.

"From what you say it's as if the whole world was primed for war and nothing could have stopped it."

"And not only could it not be stopped, we were, in our thousands, wildly and ecstatically greeting it."

"And it seems we drag God into everything, doesn't it?"

"And to make matters worse, some of the things I've seen I wouldn't blame God for avoiding."

"It's a wonder you lasted so long. And now it's my turn. Just what have I let myself in for?"

"Well, that's the odd thing. I thought they'd rejected you."

"They had, but now it seems that anyone will do. Even me with my bad chest."

"I'm sorry Howard. If I'd got back a few weeks earlier I'd have put you off it for sure, or at least done my best to."

"It seems we've all been bitten by the bug and none of us are capable of seeing through those tales of glory and duty."

"And that's the odd thing, Howard. There can't be any glory now the trenches have arrived. The only glorious one's are the fools who continue to go *over the top* and they're dying at a phenomenal rate. The others do their best to keep their heads down and wait. Wait for the Germans to charge and allow them their seconds of glory."

"Ah yes, Macaulay said something to the tune of 'the essence of war is violence, while moderation in war is imbecility'."

"There's something in that indeed. One daren't be half-hearted, though we all were at first, so sharp was the shock. And yet, it was strange that this madness rarely made us mad, except for the shell-shock. In a peculiar way it made us all the more caring, melding us all into something quite pure. Chaps you'd not bother speaking to if you'd met them in the pub, but out there we all cared for each other regardless and without question, as if by looking after one another we were taking care of ourselves. I've never encountered such comradely acts. I imagine that ultimately it is only the worst that can provoke the best from each of us. Such irony!"

"So Ally, what do the doctors say about your wounds?"

"Oh they'll heal okay, eventually. I might even rid myself of this damn stick too, in time."

"So you're quite optimistic then?"

"About the body, yes. The mind however, well that's another matter. I think we all got a little shell-shocked, regardless. I think we all went a little mad too. Life, Howard, can never be the same after this, mark my words. How could it be after going to hell and back?"

"And so, if you'd not been wounded, things still wouldn't be the same?"

"Now come on Howard, take the stars from your eyes. I told you a few minutes ago that no-one can prepare you for this war, and that is true, but it doesn't stop you from imagining, from drawing some conclusions, does it? Or are you happier with your dreams of glory?"

"Sometimes Ally, the truth appears more like a lie to the faint-hearted."

Ally never mentioned the piece of shrapnel that had

punctured his lung.

When Howard had asked about his laboured breathing he's passed it off as "a hangover from the surgery". By the time Howard returned from |Ypres, Ally had died.

# 1915 - MOBILIZATION

In August 1914 he'd been among the first of his town to go and sign up. The newspapers had made it sound so matter of fact. "Answer The Call", "You're Country Needs YOU", and spoken in the true belief that it would be "All Over By Christmas".

His mother had held her breath and had been rewarded with her son's lack thereof.

"Sorry son it's your chest. Your asthma's against you. We can't use you."

And so he continued teaching whilst witnessing the slow decline of men from the area. One by one they left never to return, or never to return the same. He'd watch them in their new, crisp uniforms parading around, receiving all the attention. Girls found the uniforms simply irresistible. Everyone seemed to be having a wild time. He'd sit in the pubs and chat to them after school. They were young, they were patriotic, they were brave and yet, Howard sensed they were also doomed. He saw the hysteria, he could touch the desire in these men, but there was more: there was the unknown; there was the unspoken question on everyone's lips - "What happens next?"

Men were being swallowed up by a thirst that this war could not quench. He read the newspapers avidly, keeping abreast of all the latest developments. "All is Well", "Victory is in Sight". General Haig was confident that the next big push would be the last. First there was Mons and then there was the Marne. Thousands were dying and the war rolled on.

He wondered why. He couldn't imagine what was going on. Newspapers were just words, but three hundred miles away, to the south east, his friends and countrymen were involved in something the like of which the world had never before witnessed. He was both appalled and intrigued at the loss of life and wondered what the truth was. What was this place that men left for and seldom returned the same; if ever? He'd heard what Ally had said, but didn't want to believe it.

By the start of 1915 the recruitment offices had become less choosy and subsequently lowered their requirements. Howard applied again hoping this time there would be a better response and was duly judged *fit for action.* His mother choked on the news, she knew she'd lost him, her only child; lost him to something more terrible than death. After a three week intensive training period at nearby Nottingham he came home awaiting his orders. They'd made him a lieutenant because he was *an educated man.*

He returned home to the same ritual he had witnessed before. Although the eyes of the girls that now found him irresistible seemed to him to be filled with a remoteness and detachment that he could only describe as haunted. Their white flesh was tired of goodbyes, and was cold to the touch. If it wasn't for the alcohol the whole sacrament would have faltered, as without this induced hysteria all concerned would have realised that they were not drinking the blood of Christ, after all; it was indeed their own.

Late in 1914 General Haig said that victory hinged on a tiny town called Ypres on the French / Belgium border area. Early in 1915 he had a similar thought, that led to the second Battle of Ypres. (The third battle would be called, ironically, Passchendaele, and again there would be no victory).

Farewells were brief and solemn: They left with twenty four hours notice, for which Howard was grateful. He was breaking his parent's hearts, he that had been granted the reprieve, but wasn't content to accept it.

They stood at the front gate together, helplessly watching him disappear into the darkness. One last time he turned and without waving he simply bowed his head to them. Turning he slipped into the night.

All day they had talked, but nothing would change his mind. He was never an obstinate man, he could find reason in most situations and was always willing to compromise, but this was somehow different; but he really didn't know why. If he could have saved his parents from this wretched day he would have, but it was unavoidable. He called it fate and he called it his duty. "I must do my bit as well, bad chest or not". But still they pleaded.

At last they would sit down together for dinner. The air was drenched with frustration, sadness and unavoidable regret: they, for what he felt he must do and he, for what his actions were doing to them. The hardest part for him was that he couldn't find the right words to acquit himself in their eyes, and at times he questioned if he really understood them himself. He promised to write and they saw him to the front gate. Both mother and father were crying uncontrollably. The last look back froze them into his memory; hanging on to each other, sobbing.

The walk to the station was only a mile, but the lead in his legs made it seem like ten. He wanted to know why he was punishing them, or was he punishing himself to punish them? His eyes barely left the ground as he forced himself on. The lights and the bustle of the station brought him back to reality. Soon he would be in the company of his men, and this in part would take his mind off his own confusion. There was just eight of them leaving on the eight o'clock to Nottingham where all the volunteers from the Midlands would congregate and travel down together on the overnight to London, and then by coach to Dover.

There was a corporal: early thirties with a face he vaguely recognised from a neighbouring town, and six privates, all boys; the eldest could only have been nineteen. He knew everyone of these faces and tears filled his eyes as he looked at them, standing to attention, so proud and expectant. He would have his hands full looking after them. He was both comforted and terrified by the prospect. Was it such a short time ago that he had taught them English? He shook his head and looked to the sky. "All that, for this… the waste, the waste". His thoughts were his own, but he wondered if the men could see it too. He made no attempt to hide his desperation, but would have denied it if any of them had asked him why, as he saluted the seven, did he look with such imploring to heaven. While the thirty minute ride to Nottingham was filled with kit checks and small talk for his men, Howard was lost in thought; about the day, his parents, and the niggling suspicion that life may never be the same again.

At Nottingham they found themselves a small part of several hundred service men all headed for the front. Howard busied himself locating the rest of his small company: twenty men and four officers. With the roll call completed and without a single absentee, they filed off to their reserved compartments on a larger train, building up steam on an adjacent platform. The air was thick with whistles, shouts and orders and suddenly, out of nowhere, came a sense of comradeship, as small units became larger and strangers became travelling companions. And as a small brass band played and loved ones waved banners and cheered, Howard caught himself smiling and joining in with the pageantry as the pains of the day began to dissipate. He hurried to the train with his men; there was a lot of catching up to do before getting into London, mid-morning the following day.

The next few days were a blur of activity and red tape followed by meetings and orders. The allied offensive was to be resumed at Ypres. Howard had never heard of the place. It appeared in small print on a large scale map and he wondered what importance a town so small could have. He wanted to ask, but didn't want to appear ignorant.

Three days after on March 13$^{th}$ 1915, after a brief ferry crossing from Dover, Howard set foot on war-torn, French soil. Although a more accurate description would have been French mud. The winter of 1914/15 had seen some of the wettest months for years. In Calais it wasn't too bad, but on the 40 miles or so to Ypres, the roads were treacherous. It took the best part of a day to cover the distance.

He'd left Britain, a country at war, but a country without war on its soil. Now he was in France, a matter of miles from home and he had to make immediate adjustments. This was hard. How could he prepare for such contrasts? His stomach hollowed. The air smelt different, while the light from a cloudy sky hung trembling over the sea and countryside. He looked about him, watching the activity: The unloading of men and machines, the supplies. Men as far as the eye could see attempting to gain some order within the chaos.

"Seventy Fifth?" A captain standing at the bottom of the gangplank was calling hopefully. "Good to see you… been waiting long? Good, okay, now follow me and we'll get you out of here in no time."

The small troupe followed the captain obediently, weaving their way through the mazes of activity. Although the crossing had been uneventful and the sea calm, the quayside was littered with vomit.

"Nervous men in strange surroundings awaiting the unknown," thought Howard, as he did his best to avoid the numerous pools.

"Bit of a shock to the system, what?"

Howard nodded, tasting his own bile rising to a dry mouth. He swallowed hard and for now the moment was over.

"We've got transport for you just over here," the captain pointed over to a mud-splattered machine.

"You'll get all of us into that?" Howard questioned incredulously.

"One way or another, yes." The captain sounded confident.

Two hours later men and supplies were loaded, and the convoy, that consisted of twelve similarly overloaded trucks, began its journey to the front.

The captain handed Howard his orders in a small, brown envelope marked with an 'R'.

"R?" Questioned Howard.

"Reconnaissance, old man. You've got the interesting job!" Joked the captain.

Howard looked around at the other faces and nobody else was laughing.

"Interesting?"

"Certainly. It means you'll be able to get about more. None of all that hanging around. It's the boredom that does it for most men."

Howard decided not to ask further questions. Here he was on his first real day of duty, sporting an officer's uniform, but with no idea whatsoever as to what the job entailed. He'd been taught how to clean and fire his revolver, thrust a bayonet into a bail of straw and the bare minimum of first aid. There would be no acclimatizing to the situation, they'd simply arrive and start doing whatever soldier's did in war, right from the word go. And from nowhere would come the desire to kill or maim any and all that stood in his way?

"Look out there!" Howard shouted and a pathway opened up for him, leading to the back of the truck. He barely got there in time. He felt his insides lurch in a grinding spasm, and a yard from the back he started to spit the acidic contents of his stomach out the back of the covered truck. On his knees, with eyes closed, and head hanging over the flap, he continued to retch. In his mind he was nine years old, crouched over a small tin bowl, feeling the chill of fever. A hand was on his forehead and the reassuring voice of his mother could be heard, telling him, "I'm here, you're all right now."

"You all right sir?" He heard a young voice behind him say.

Slowly his eyes opened and watched as the muddied road bounced under him, as the truck bumped and jolted along. He turned in the direction of the voice and through his tearing eyes he could see someone handing him something. He stared, mouth open, dribbling.

"Handkerchief sir.. Thought you might like to, er…"

It was one of the young privates.

"Tha… thanks…most kind of you… thanks."

He turned away to wipe his mouth and face and saw Calais disappearing as they climbed out of the valley. He was shaking. It felt like all he knew was fading into the past and was fast being replaced by an unknown, black emptiness. He prayed he was wrong.

# THE TRIP TO YPRES: MARCH 14^(TH) 1915

"At least it's better than walking." Chimed the captain.

"Walking?!" Howard thought. "Walking?"

Thinking the captain was enjoying a joke at his expense, Howard swung round to confront him, but before he could say a word he became aware of the real message. The captain was standing behind him a few feet away and pointing with his baton, his face etched in genuine concern. Had he been oblivious to these men, or had they just appeared, dragging themselves along the side of the road? Faces grim and tired, some blackened by fire or explosion. Some limped while comrades supported others. They were quiet, not caring about anything other than keeping slowly moving.

"Just not enough trucks to go around. Think yourselves fortunate to be Recon."

Howard said nothing and turned his gaze back to the road. Back to the faces, to the tattered bags of uniforms. "And this mud… it's everywhere… on everything." He whispered to himself.

At best the truck managed about ten to fifteen miles an hour. Numerous times they all had to get out and push the thing when the mud seemed to act more like snow and deny them traction on the slightest incline. It overheated twice and once became waterlogged during a cloudburst necessitating a thorough clean of the engine by the meticulous driver / mechanic.

The landscape was a sodden wilderness. Rolling and desolate and from a sky of torn and angry clouds a steady rain fell. The trip lasted seven and a half, desperate hours. Howard tried to sleep, but was content to lie, eyes closed, feigning sleep for most of the way. His mouth tasted vile, his body still shook. He was first hot then cold. He wanted to scream and wake from the nightmare.

Gradually the sound of gunfire became audible and as it began to get dark the flashes of the explosions could be seen, far off on the horizon. The hollowness in his stomach lurched increasingly as the blasts got increasingly louder and louder.

Camp was a collection of tents, about 50 or so, haphazardly arranged. From a distance hundreds of men scurried around like ants, but they were noiseless, drowned out by the heavy guns.

The captain introduced Howard to his CO, a major who appeared, thankfully, a rational and concerned man. His orders were simple: "As soon as you and your men have located your tents and settled in, report back here and we'll get you up to the front. We've had little in the way of Recon lately, since the others left. Had to let them go you know, they'd almost had it! Had expected your crew sooner. Oh well, can't be helped."

"Will the major be orienting us himself?" Howard was more than aware that his 'crew' was made up of all but raw recruits.

"Probably have to skip that. I'll let you have a couple of guides until you get used to the terrain. Other than that you get a free hand. Information's the thing... can't win a war without Recon!" Then without warning he took Howard aside.

"Sorry old man. It's madness here... but keep it to yourself. There's about a million men over there in that direction," he said pointing to the flashes in the blackening sky, "All races, denominations and creeds, not to mention the languages. They arrive there, at the front, as a unit, but with the advances and the retreats things get a little... er, let's say, mixed up, with all those trenches looking remarkably similar. You get the picture? Just do your best, son... Do your best. Show them to the tents captain." At which he tipped his hat with his baton and sheepishly retired to his tent.

"Right away, sir. Okay, follow me you men."

Obediently, the unit fell in and followed the captain. They were headed in the direction of a cluster of tents, each about ten feet square.

"Okay chaps, this will be your home for the foreseeable future. It's not much, but at least you don't have to slum it in the trenches like the rest. Straighten the place up a bit, dump your belongings and report back to HQ in say, twenty minutes. Good."

The officers took one tent while the men split up and occupied the others. All things considered, they all agreed it could have indeed been a lot worse.

Inside the officer's tent there were two kerosene lamps that popped away like boiling kettles as they burned and threw long, yellow-stained shadows around the tent. There were four beds, two metal chests of drawers, a slightly unsteady hat and coat stand and a small collection of tin bowls, jugs, cups, plates and a selection of basic cutlery.

"Home sweet home." Sighed Howard as he threw his pack on the nearest bed and collapsed in a heap beside it. "Home sweet home. Huh! Anybody else got anything to say?"

He looked around at his fellow officers and waited.

"Nothing? Nothing at all?"

"Wouldn't do any good to moan, I guess?" Came a voice from the darker side of the tent. "What's the use of worrying, it never was worthwhile. So, pack up your troubles in your old kit bag and smile, smile, smile!!" By the last line all four were shouting the words of the song at the top of their voices. Then it went very quiet, and silently they eyed each other.

"I really don't know what to say. I know I want to say something, but I open my mouth and the words won't come…"

"It's a bloody mess, and it'll kill us."

Don't mention death, Bach, it's bad luck you know. A Welsh voice joined in.

"Will somebody fall the men in and get things going here. I've had enough waiting. Let's get on with the war."

They all sprang up and filed out into the cool, night air.

Back at HQ, which consisted of a tent four times the size of their own, with far superior furniture, the major and captain awaited the four officers.

"Ah, there you are. Get them all drinks, please, Jones." The major had his own batman, a tall skinny chap in a spotless white shirt and jacket with a dickey-bow and black trousers, pressed to perfection.

The major led them to a large table and as they sipped their drinks he did his best to explain the current situation, with baton and map, without hiding his frustration at the inadequate communications and his abiding hatred of "this confounded trench warfare".

"It's turned into a battle of attrition, nothing more. A battle of waiting to see who gets frustrated first. And then one of ours sticks his head out to see if Fritz is up to anything and 'crack', he's on the floor of the trench with half his head missing… and so it grinds on. Then we send over some mortars and they do the same. But everyone's tucked away snugly in their trenches, so it has no effect… running and hiding… bloody stalemate!"

Half an hour later the troop was in the field. The front was about five miles away to the northwest and the truck would ferry them most of the way. Each officer was assigned five men, and the major's sector, an area of about twenty square miles, was divided into four giving each group a sizeable territory to be responsible for. Their task was to go out each night for as long as it took to record who was in what trench and where. A simple enough task on paper, but with the next big push expected within a month or so, time was of the essence.

Without warning the truck lurched to a halt. Twenty four shadowy figures with blackened faces leapt from the back and made their way in the direction of a similar figure, swinging a lantern, fifty yards away.

"We'll see you back here at six. Good luck and keep your heads down." The captain shouted from the cab of the truck.

The shadowy figure with the lantern greeted Howard warmly.

"Evening sir, welcome." He said as he saluted. "Corporal Timms, $5^{th}$ Lancs, good to have Recon back again. Follow me, it's about a mile."

The big guns had been silent for a while now, and except for occasional rifle fire and flares, everything was pretty dark and quiet. The landscape appeared fairly flat with light scrub and the occasional, blackened tree. They were following what seemed to be a well-worn track leading to a large mound in the distance. They sloshed their way noisily through the mud. As they got nearer, the mound turned magically into a bustling, underground HQ.

They passed through barbed wire fences guarded by sentries who eyed the party with rehearsed suspicion. They followed Timms down into the belly of the mound. Each unit was given a map, a guide and told to "get out there and familiarize yourselves with your sectors".

Before they split up into their groups Howard took the guides aside.

"Look, I don't know what you've been told, but we're all pretty raw you know. We just arrived this evening, and Recon has come as a bit of a surprise to us."

"That's all right sir, we only got here five days ago ourselves." Replied a smiling cockney private.

"But the job… it's pretty important just to hand over to a an inexperienced unit…"

"Don't worry sir, this time tomorrow you'll be bloomin' experts. Let's go."

Bewildered, Howard glanced at his watch then checked his revolver. It was 8.35pm on March 14$^{th}$, 1915. His war had begun.

# LETTER HOME: YPRES, MARCH 19<sup>TH</sup>, 1915.

My dearest Mother and Father,

You have known me as a man of words. Today I am less than that. The events of the past few weeks serve to remind me that we can only know what we know and above that we can only imagine. To imagine war before one takes part in it is impossible. Coming here I tried to prepare myself by way of imagining, and now I am happy to report that on the subject of war I have no imagination whatsoever. It's as if hell had opened up and swallowed us.

We had our 'baptism of fire' on the 14<sup>th</sup>, and although it was thankfully uneventful, I became aware of the changes war makes to a man.

There are twenty four in our unit with most of the *men* being boys, and most of the boys ex-pupils from St Thomas's. That night I felt real fear, but I suspect even that will get worse. Conversely, all the boys in my unit appeared to *light up* in the presence of danger. They drew their revolvers (we have no rifles as we have been assigned Recon duty, and rifles would only hamper us in our task), and ceased at that second to be the boys they were. Whatever it was; hate, fear, exhilaration, I don't know, but it was as if they had crossed the barrier of manhood in a second's, mysterious initiation. There was no ancient rite, as such, other than an obvious desire to survive. There were no stories around a camp fire. We just let them loose and they became potential killers. And I am appalled. I had expected some, or all of them, to run at the first opportunity, but quite the reverse. A shell exploded some fifty yards away throwing mud and shrapnel within feet of us. The boys simply dived to the floor and acted like veterans.

That was the closest we got to action, which allowed us the chance to acquaint ourselves with *the Front,* which sounds dramatic, but is really just a vast rabbit warren of trenches filled to bursting with our young men. At twenty four I feel like an old man at times!

I've never known mud like it is here; It has a life of its own somehow. It becomes an entity that sucks, grabs and wearies all who attempt to move in it. It absorbs my will... And of course, it STINKS!! (The ground is also our lav). And not only that, the ground is a tomb. We've heard it said that only a few months ago when the battle was at it fiercest, the men who were shot and fell, became part of the cover for the survivors. And it's not unusual to see hands and feet protruding from the trench walls!

It seems that in order to survive here one has to become inhuman. To kill without conscience or be killed without regret. This is the simplicity of war: Forget you exist and pretty soon you won't.

Oh Father, they said there was dignity here! How they lied.

When we returned after that first mission, just after sun-up, we came straight back to our tent, which is the only saving grace of our existence, and without washing or eating I threw myself on the bed and slept a fitful, but none the less, blessed sleep. And this will be my only release from the battle for who knows how long.

I hope this letter finds you well and I pray God keeps us safe until we meet again. Please pray for me, as I feel that my prayers alone may not be sufficient.

I've seen little glory here, only mud and death. There are no answers, only countless questions. There is not even an enemy, only men's pride.

My Love - As Always, Howard.

PS Please keep my letters as they will survive if for any reason my journal doesn't...

# JOURNAL: MARCH 31<sup>ST</sup>, 1915.

In a way it was like a dream in the way that it happened. And yet, in a totally different way, it was worse than any nightmare. But even that does not do the horror of it all justice. It was like touching a boiling kettle and not instantly, and involuntarily removing one's hand, but keeping it there until the feeling became numb. I was a rabbit mesmerised at night in the beam of a torchlight, frozen to the spot and unable to move. It should have been easy to turn away or simply put my hands to my eyes and yet, it was the disbelief that kept me watching. In all, it was the dream we have all had where we want to run, but some unseen force stills our legs and heightens our fear and vulnerability.

It was just before dawn and our group was slowly approaching HQ; about a mile away. We were all very tired after having spent almost eight hours in the field logging the trenches. The weather for once wasn't too bad although the snow that had fallen two nights ago still remained in patches, keeping the earth firm, and not the usual quagmire it has been since we arrived. To the east the night sky was turning from a black to a faintly clouded, blue-tinged morning when, without warning, we heard the whistles. The whistles that signified that somewhere in the clearing light about 250 yards away, our troops were about to go over the top. Checking my watch I realised that we were twenty minutes late in returning from our patrol and very shortly we could be unwilling bystanders, or at worst, participants, to a surprise push from our troops.

And out they poured, silently running, seeking the best from the element of surprise, which lasted at best for twenty seconds. At which, canons roared, flares went up and as the German machine guns tore into their murderous chatter, our party dived to the ground for cover. Our troops continued to appear, like magic, from the darkness of the trenches into the sporadically lit arena where, like animated toy soldiers, they danced with their last breaths.

I wanted to shout; to warn them. I wanted to stand up and stop it all, but all I could do was lie there and watch while men, acting for little more than target practice, slumped and twisted into contorted piles of twitching uniforms in *no-man's land*. I told myself that this was war and I should accept it, but I couldn't take it in, it was ridiculous... these were men, human beings, and some we must have had dinner with last night.

The push lasted for three or four minutes. It was probably a speculative act just to see if the Germans were still awake, as I couldn't see that any other purpose existed.

After a minute or so the whistles sounded the *all clear* and I immediately motioned for our group to head in the direction of this recent carnage. We sprinted directly to the trenches where minutes before the troops had emerged, intending to organise a stretcher party and do something, anything, for the open-mouthed, faced in the mud, heaps of dead and dying men, moaning and writhing within easy reach.

We were however told that the snipers would pick us off if we tried. So we called to the wounded, telling them to keep still and to hang on for daylight. When the murky light finally arrived we fled out under a white flag and finally retrieved fourteen wounded out of an initial force of 180.

Back at HQ I sat alone in the mess hall, reliving the horror, that continued whether my eyes were open or shut - the faces, the cries and the stench.

For some reason my mind went back to when I was nine or ten, when a group of us boy scouts went camping out on the Peaks. It was the first time I had been away from home without my parents. It was the third day with eight to go and I was putting a brave face on things, but I was feeling terribly, so desperately, homesick. Three days previous I couldn't have imagined feeling so bad that I would have to go out into the countryside, away from the masters and the other boys, just to cry unseen.

Tonight had been vaguely similar, I reasoned. I had just had my sensibilities torn from my body, my heart ached, my stomach lurched, and I was a million miles from home. The one thing missing was a quiet and secluded part of the Peaks where I could go and cry, and be by myself, and in some way recover from all this.

And then I thought of the dead and the dying and I was immediately ashamed; though the feelings still linger and the images are now etched into my memory.

# LETTER HOME, APRIL 21$^{ST}$, 1915.

My Dearest Mother and Father,

I am unsure how I should start this letter, as so much has happened, both *here* at the Front, and *in here*, inside me. But first, how are you both?

As I write I can see the parlour in half-light with you sitting together, opening this letter. Outside, the day is slowly drawing to dusk and there is rain scratching at the windows from the perpetual gray sky. The lights are on and the fire crackles and pops; spitting dampness from the logs. The smell of cooking is seeping from the kitchen - dinner will be ready soon. A voice calls, "Be sure to wash your hands before dinner." I come running in from the garden, my wet shoes slipping and sliding on the stone kitchen floor, and plunge my cold hands into hot water. I have spent the afternoon playing with friends in the nearby woods. I am eight years old. "Didn't I tell you to put on your coat? And look at your shoes, what a mess. Go right up those stairs and get into the bath".

Always at odds for no reason. But isn't that what boys are meant to do, get dirty? There was a time I'm sure that you thought that I only misbehaved just to annoy you and to get your attention. I had overheard a conversation that went, "I swear he does it just to get under my skin." How wrong you were. And if you could see me today you'd realise that. The game is no longer soccer as I crouch here in a trench wanting desperately to be back home. My uniform is sodden with blood, rain and mud, thicker than any soccer field I ever played on, and the blood hasn't trickled from a cut knee.

My watch says 3am: your old watch, father. It still works, though the face is scratched, and in those scratches lies the Belgian mud, ground into the glass. I am still shaking, but not from the cold... though it is colder than death in here. For now all is quiet and I hear nothing but the ringing in my ears and a desperate voice in my head crying to be freed from all this. How I long to be back in Melton for the spring.

We set out at eight last night on our usual sortie; filling in the blanks for HQ. All went well until about 12:15am, when the heavens opened with canon and mortar fire. Until then the night had been uneventful with only the usual level of firing that kept both our, and their, heads down. We leapt into a bomb crater and before we could find any cover a mortar exploded about twenty feet away on the rim of the crater. A light flashed for a split second illuminating the faces of the boys around me. And when I close my eyes now, that's all I see: that look of surprise mingled with fear and anticipation. Eyes, for an instant, just slits, parted lips, and teeth clenched, braced for the impact...

I remember looking at my watch. It was 1:55am. I was gasping for air and there seemed to be a pressure on my chest that felt like a ton weight. I lay there on my back in the darkness, wheezing and coughing, regaining my senses. The smoky-air hung like ghosts around me. And these phantoms had lives of their own as they danced loosely in the light of the occasional flares. Slowly, as my eyes adjusted to the darkness, I gazed about me. The view to my right was blocked by something, above me there were the shadows and to my left, again my view was blocked. A chill ran through my body and with it came the immediate desire to break free from whatever was on me. I raised myself on my elbows and the weight on my chest seemed to roll down to my thighs. I panicked, and leaping up I shrieked, as if startled from sleep. As I knelt there, holding whatever breath I could, a flare went up close by, and in the quivering light lay five, motionless bodies forming what had been a protective barrier around me; contorted, gruesome, silent and blind-eyed. I screamed again, maybe hoping to wake them. Back in the darkness again I fumbled to my left and found a face. My fingers trembled as I followed the contours and gently ran my fingers through the hair. In my horror I wanted to scream again, but nothing came out. I tried again, confused, but once more I was mute. Gulping for air, my head began to swim; my whole, kneeling body started to shake and rock. I gagged, choked, then spluttered vomit into the darkness, not caring where. I thought, "If this is the end, God, then let it happen, I don't care anymore." And I began to sob in a low moan that came from a place I never knew existed. It was as if I was connected to the earth by my knees, and from the roots swelled up such a surge of despair that it felt like the unified misery of the world was being channelled solely through my nervous system. Without a thought I leapt to my feet and unbridling the revolver at my side and charged up the bank of the crater brandishing the weapon while attempting to scream once more, at the top of my voice. I hadn't gone more than ten paces before I heard gunfire. Bullets whistled close by, and then a voice sounded, "Cease fire, cease fire, he's one of ours." I stumbled to a halt and looked out into the gloom. My arms fell limp at my sides and the revolver fell to the ground. My body became a mass of raw nerves that shook every muscle into disjointed motion, like a puppet on elastic strings.

"Quick, grab him, before they finish him off."

From nowhere strong arms picked me up and swiftly brought me to the safety of this trench, where I now lie, writing to you. They say I collapsed and slept for over twenty four hours. They're sending me back to England. They say I might have shell shock.

My Love, Howard.

# AS THE REALITY SANK IN

At 25 part of him felt like a well-rounded, seasoned veteran and something of an old man. But hadn't he gone to war and hadn't it been more horrific than even he could have imagined? He had seen his pupils murdered before his very eyes. Hadn't he witnessed the whole, futile madness; and all in a matter of weeks? How could men bear to be there indefinitely, or as he saw it, until they finally succumbed to shell, bullet or bayonet? War was a death sentence, but what he wondered, had his generation done to deserve it? Regardless of what side one was on, no-one could ignore the already catastrophic casualties: he was remembering when they had over-run the enemy trenches and had used the bodies they found there to fortify the crumbling walls. Didn't these young men also have families and loved ones nervously waiting at home for news of their fate? It was obvious for Howard to see that war was not glorious, as he had been promised, because without honour, how could there be glory? In fact, just as Ally had described. Yes, he wanted the allies to be triumphant, and yes, he felt he was on the side of right: but how right? All he felt he really had on his side was the cause: the fending off of an hostile aggressor. But being on the side of good also meant being as bad as the enemy at times - "All is fair in love and war". It was a continuation of the thinking he had put into practice so often at school in an effort to motivate pupils. Subtle suggestions that 'you are as quick as the slowest among you' and 'you are as strong as your weakest link', that led unavoidably to 'you are only as good as the most evil one of you'.

Little by little the system was draining away his dignity until all those concerned would feel the same, and be prepared to go to the same, desperate extremes to justify the end.

It also occurred to him that this was the first war where men were playing a secondary role to the weapons they used, which appeared to be amplified by the adoption of the trenches. There was a saying amongst the men that 'you'll never see the bullet that kills you', and he knew exactly what it meant. Before, in say the Franco-Prussian War or the Crimea, generally speaking, all could be remarkably even between the opposing sides. There was cannon, sword and rifle, but the day was won or lost as a result of close combat. All was now changing. Both sides could now kill from a distance, with no conscience. With the refinement and improvement of the weapons being the reason. In this war there would be less hand to hand combat, fewer cavalry charges. The killing would be done at a comfortable distance; and it was surprising how little one felt as mortar after mortar was fired at a distant enemy with unknown quantities of men, waiting an anonymous death.

It was obscene, callous and inhuman. And honour. Where was the honour?

And now there was the malevolence of poison gas that had entered his unsuspecting and unconscious lungs; carried in the very air he breathed. For Howard, this was the final insult: the final slap in a long line of painful slaps in the face. At this point, even victory began to sound hollow.

But how would a war like this end? When one side literally runs out of men to die? And of course, how would the victor feel at winning such a war? Surely, nothing approaching pride: at best it could only be relief, from the continuous and pointless slaughter.

And finally, how could peace retain its true meaning when the definition of war had sunk so low?

Howard wondered if there would be a *real* peace

again, with the victor now filled with the same horror, disgust and fear as the vanquished? There were too many questions, too many loose ends...

As yet there seemed to be little hope of the war being won *in a few months*, as were the early predictions from both sides, and already the newspapers were calling it - THE WAR TO END ALL WARS.

He thought of his brief experience and wondered if the whole world might not end up being the wasteland that large parts of Belgium and France now were: just mud, with blackened, skeletal trees, bereft of even the bird's singing. Not only was it man against man, but now, ironically, all men against nature. And looking out over what must have been green fields and hills, he had felt his heart sink. And somewhere in that sinking feeling he knew exactly how it would be to die an unnatural, war-death, in a foreign land: the nightmare of being lost forever in a sea of mud. Of being trampled underfoot and to finally dissolve back into the earth.

Recently, the literary world had been captivated by the poetry of Rupert Brooke and in particular his poem, Soldier, that began with the words:

If I should die think only this of me;
That there's some corner of a foreign field
That is forever England.

There was for Howard something inexplicably disturbing, yet moving, about those lines: and ironically, something that neither man would fully understand, or indeed, experience.

Brooke had been to the Front in 1914 and survived. He was on his way to the Dardanelles in April 1915 when he had died of blood poisoning and was buried on the island of Skyros in Greece. Prophetic words indeed, (all but the context of death). Howard had also been to the Front and survived, and these lines became as familiar to him as if he had written them himself. In fact, for Howard the poem did only consist of those three lines. He was not an emphatically, patriotic man. He believed he was first, part of humanity before being, accidentally, British. And so he could conclude that there were indeed corners of foreign fields that would be forever France, Russia, Germany, Scotland, Wales, Serbia, Ireland, Turkey, Austria, Australia and New Zealand, as well as England. It was for the *Soldier* and not just the English Soldier that his heart sank. And regardless of whether the Soldier died or returned home, he would ultimately leave, symbolically, his blood or tears: it was the experience alone that made the foreigner, native.

Howard had written poetry throughout his life and had actively not written anything related to his time spent near Ypres. But there was something about those few, short lines of Rupert Brooke's that unleashed something in him that made the writing about such primal experiences compulsory. What he had witnessed he had believed was his to keep as a voiceless memory; a dignified silence: but not now. He wanted to tell everyone about his ordeal and maybe save his sanity in doing so:

> There is something I would share
> That is locked away in silence,
> For no-one to hear again.
>
> Timidly I cry
> As I catch myself returning
> To that night, when,
> For an instant,
> Time stood still to ask me
> If I could go on.

Time told me
That if I chose to continue
There would be no reward,
Only silence.

I had gone there
Neither to fight nor die;
There was little reason for either.
More, I was swept along
By the frightening tide of patriotism
That threatens to divide the world forever.

I awoke too late to realise
We were not fighting for freedom or peace,
But merely for gain.

I am cheated and deceived, but what of it?
There were thousands that never asked why,
But followed, regardless.

After me,
My silence is theirs.
And yours is what is left.

# JOURNAL: MAY 1915

I cannot say truly what it is, but I believe we are all decidedly up to our necks in it, together. And to deny this would be both cowardly and insane. This is not about living, dying or being wounded; neither is it about patriotism, fear nor shame. This is about offering one's self up to the possible eventuality of any of these six choices. Sometimes I even believe that events can get so wrong, that after a while they start to look right - somehow. Is this blind optimism? Is this denial? Maybe this is all, and more.

Cheating death has left me feeling immortal. I have been saved for some reason. The next time, and I feel somehow that there will be a next time, I shall not carry a gun. I will simply serve my brothers and not the munitions factories or the politicians. If they'll have me, I'll cook the food, push the pen or carry the stretcher: but don't ask me to kill.

# JOURNAL: MAY 1915

Two weeks have passed already since they sent me back. Yesterday I went to Nottingham for a check-up and the news was just about what I expected. Mentally I am recovering from the shock. They say it will be a slow process and that I must live life 'one day at a time', as my mood can change dramatically, and sometimes with no warning at all. The smallest thing can either depress me or pick me up. 'Melancholy' they say. The doctor's though, are more concerned about my physical health. It appears that on the fateful night the German's were using poison gas, which makes those

'ghosts' even more sinister. The gas has affected my already asthmatic lungs, causing perhaps, permanent damage. As yet I can't feel anything other than an irritating tickle of a cough, but they say it could develop into something worse in the future. They didn't say what, but they will continue to do regular tests.

For me the hardest part is the depression. It manifests itself as an unidentified emptiness down in my gut area: Which feels dark and ominous. It swells as I breathe and seems to have a life of its own. On occasions it disappears for hours and then, for no apparent reason, seems to jolt back into place.

I think a lot about the boys. I have filled my dreams with their dead faces and I wake, heart pounding, wondering why I was spared. I go over it, time and again in my mind and it still makes no sense; as if I could find some reason in war. But they were so unafraid by it all. I think that maybe the dead know when their time is near and somehow aren't affected by the same fear as the rest of us. Well, that's what I tell myself in the hope that what they suffered was lessened by some innate calm and spiritual awareness. Next month there is to be a memorial service for them, and their families have asked me to be there and say a few words, if I'm up to it. I am both honoured and mortified. Did I not lead them to their deaths?

So much has happened, so much to take in. Writing a journal is a way of keeping up with the events. I hope to live long enough to look back and read them and maybe make more sense of all this madness: Maybe, *ultimate sense.* It's so hard to take stock of situations when they continue to unravel. I hope that when this war is long over we may find a silver lining that at present doesn't exist. And even though I was at the Front only a matter of weeks the adjustments I had to make in every area of life were endless. And I am appalled to think that there are men living out there, as best they can, denying their shock, sadness and outrage at what is expected of them all day, every day. And back at home only the good news is being printed in the newspapers. Such a dangerous dichotomy.

The stories of German atrocities in Belgium have stirred up such hate, but how can people here, who haven't experienced the desperate and irrational side of war, believe that it is only 'them' who are capable of such acts? Do they think that only the enemy has the ability to kill and maim? And what of us? Are we merely returning fire and defending ourselves or do we also have an aggressive nature - a dark side? We say we are defending democracy and freedom. We say God is on our side. But who says so? Surely not God? Can anyone believe a God, such as our God, would support such mindless and brutal acts?

And yet, when all is said and done, I feel a desperate connection with those men and boys. I sensed, during those days of scurrying around in the dark, sliding and sticking in that ever present mud, that something special, almost spiritual, was taking place. It may sound strange, but the inhuman aspects of war not only promoted a definite sense of caring and community; breaking down class barriers and the like. But I also believe I recognised something quite primal in our collective behaviour. Earlier I mentioned men and boys, as if there was some division between the two. Originally, because I knew the majority of the boys as pupils, that was how I perceived them: but I was wrong. In a way we were all boys, all of us who had never before *taken up arms.*

After the first couple of days there was a marked impression within us all that we had proven ourselves, that we had done our bit and survived - and we had come through. It was like the ancient initiation rites when a boy would be taken from his family at a certain age, away from the influence of his mother, to learn, in the company of older, wiser men, what was expected of him as a man. He would learn to hunt, kill, use a knife, to familiarize himself with the forests and all that lived and grew there. In short he would take on the responsibility of *Manhood:* something I believe we, at the start of the twentieth century, have long forgotten. Everything today is industry and we run the risk of selling our souls to the pursuit of ends that are purely and above all soullessly, materialistic.

I have always loved and respected nature: didn't we evolve from nature ourselves? And lying there in the Belgian mud I imagined I was in a way returning to the earth, as so many would literally do. And during those times when we couldn't for one reason or another, return to our tents at HQ, we would sit in the trenches, sometimes for hours, waiting. Waiting for darkness, waiting for light, waiting for orders, waiting for food… And we just sat and slept, wrote letters, sang, told jokes or just daydreamed. And as I looked around at the men in their mud-soaked uniforms they seemed to blend in with their surroundings, until they became faces peering out from the walls. And twenty feet below, in the bowels of the earth, were the sleeping quarters. How cosy this felt in a warm, subterranean burrow far from the thought of war: rabbits in a burrow, such was my connection to the earth.

Today I walked out and once again became one with nature. Sometimes I believe I'll die out here, such is the affinity I feel. I would have liked to walk further, but I'm still a bit shaky and mother worries when I'm gone too long. And so I idled down the back lane, over the stile and out onto the moor to sit in thought.

I can't break free from this war: something out there wants me as much as I need *it*. I wish I understood myself better. I know it has something to do with mortality, but conversely, nothing to do with death. I think I want to be of service, to help… There must be something more that I can do…?

The weather was fine, a bit breezy, but fresh and spring-like. Down in the valley bluebells were clearly visible and the air smelled of wild garlic. Spring is such a hopeful time of year: the annual genesis and a time of promise. I wonder how I shall age? Will I be just like father?

Back at home lunch was almost ready when some visitors arrived: a small deputation from school. Two girls and two boys from my 4$^{th}$ year English class, armed with flowers and a card. The card reads as if I am some returning hero and I am touched that I am missed. The headmaster, Mr Rogers, who brought the children, a socially awkward but well-meaning man of about sixty, walked me out into the garden and re-assured me that I should take as long as necessary to recuperate. They have brought a temporary teacher in, so my classes are covered. I thanked him and he shook me fiercely by the hand and left without saying what I knew to be on his mind. I fancy he was unsure about whether or not to enquire too deeply as to my 'recent,... er... misfortunes'. Why are we English so damned polite? I turned and called after him...

"Everything's going to be all right, you know."

He turned, and without appearing to think, he replied,

"Yes... thought it would be. Well done old man, well done... We're all very proud of you, you know."

After lunch I returned to bed. Mother and father sat with me for a while until I dozed off and then woke again at ten. The house was quiet and dark and every step creaked as I tiptoed downstairs to make this entry in my journal. I sat and enjoyed the dying embers of a once healthy fire. Today is a celebration for being alive. Slightly south from where I sit, drinking tea and sucking on an empty pipe, men are barely living recognizable lives, and something inside of me wants to share it with them... once more.

# MAY 22$^{ND}$ 1915

"Ah Howard, good to see you, come in please."

Dr Clifford Manning MD welcomed his new patient with the customary shake of the hand. It was their first meeting.

"Thank you doctor."

"Take a seat please. So how are things?"

"Difficult to say at present... hoped you might help me out there."

Their eyes met and the doctor returned the knowing smile and then looked back down at his desk.

"Exactly, yes. Then let me reword a little... You see I have your medical report here and very little else, and if I am to help you in any way I feel I should be honest, totally honest with you."

"Thank you, I'd appreciate that."

Howard started to feel a little uncomfortable. Why shouldn't he be honest, he thought.

"You're not in uniform then?"

"No. I didn't think it was quite suitable, all things considered".

"You're probably right... So tell me, what's the latest with your lungs?"

"Well, there's better news on that subject. I heard yesterday that although they will never be as good as they were before... before the gassing, and although they will be weaker and susceptible to infection, it seems they believe they are not as badly damaged as was first thought".

"Well that's good news at least. A beastly and cowardly business that gassing".

"You said you would reword that question. What is it you want to know?"

"Yes, thank you... Your medical report also

contains your psychological report. It doesn't tell me very much. It gives me jargon, but very little else".

"You spoke of honesty, total honesty. What did you mean by that?"

Manning looked hard at Howard, then glanced out of the window to the busy streets of Nottingham, four floors below.

"Is this honesty so bad?"

There was a pause.

"You have to understand Howard that all this is very new. New to me and new to the medical world in general. In fact I've barely completed my training".

Manning smiled again at Howard, raising his eyebrows and shaking his head.

"You mean you can't help?"

"It isn't that, it's more a question of identification. You see, I can examine your body and make a diagnosis based on the knowledge we have today. But when we begin to discuss your mind, well... there just isn't the same amount of information available in order to make any kind of serious diagnosis. You are among my first psychological patients and, I have to be honest, this situation preys upon my Hippocratic Oath".

"Meaning what exactly?"

"Meaning that you and I are to go where neither of us has been before. Out there somewhere, into the darkness of time. And the responsibility I feel is immense".

"Doctor Manning, I am touched. Not only by your honesty, but also with your humility. I am starting to feel safer and I thank you for that. But tell me, what can I expect from this... I think they call it... the *talking cure*?"

"Yes, the talking cure. Well, there is a Doctor Forsyth who started the first clinic in London in 1913 and he's doing well. And again there's a Doctor Rivers near Edinburgh who's beginning to do remarkable things. However, they are the exceptions. Generally speaking this hysteria, melancholy, whatever you want to call it, is being treated with an indifference that at times borders on the punitive".

"I'm not sure what you mean…?"

"Meaning that it is easier to be cruel when dealing with something, that is for now, not fully understood. Meaning that today, all over the country, men are being shamed into *getting better*".

"And what are you intending to do to me?"

"I intend to set you free from the mental anguish you are experiencing with the limited knowledge I possess. Dr Freud, a man I am sure you have heard of is, as far as I am concerned, a genius, and with his lead I'm sure we will find a way".

# JOURNAL: MAY 22$^{ND}$ 1915

I believe I have been most fortunate in being selected for treatment with Dr Manning. He appears sensitive with a degree of humility one doesn't often find in the professional field. Almost at once I was at ease and then we appeared to be of one voice - so to speak. If I didn't know any better, I'd believe he said considerably more than is normal, especially considering it was our first meeting. And quite apart from me telling him of my problems, which he seemed to understand, he also reciprocated with details of his own life, which at first I thought quite odd... Odd, but in a kindly way.

He started out by telling me about his decision to start this psychological training, which it appears hinged solely on his only son, Ernest, joining up in 1914. Or more to the point, after he received the first letter from him, from somewhere on the Western Front. The horror he felt after reading this letter made him sign up for the training, as he couldn't imagine what he could do for his son if he was 'struck down', similarly to me. He went on further by saying that he felt somewhat responsible for Ernest joining up, what with all the pomp, ceremony and national pride. But now all he could think of was getting Ernest back, in light of what he had seen and heard in his own consulting room, and of course what he'd read in the letters.

The poor man is racked with guilt and terrified at the thought of what might become of his son.

It seems also that his wife has changed from being a very out-going and confident woman, into someone who spends her hours in constant worry. She never strays far from the telephone and freezes each time a letter drops through the door.

I wonder if he tells all his patients similar stories, or is it just me? I don't mean to sound egotistic, but I do feel a close bond to this man.

This is surely a strange thing. Somehow, both here and in France, there is a clear desire for honesty and camaraderie. I must mention this to Dr Manning when we meet next.

# 1915: SO FAR

For the remainder of his life 1915 would be the year that Howard would return to time and again for questioning, sustenance and reason.

After all it was the year that he had been just inches away from being blown apart by a mortar shell. And then, only months later, when he had recovered sufficiently to take up his job again, his pendulum would swing, without warning, in totally the other direction: He would fall in love, for the first time.

Where the idea came from he wasn't sure, but as he was ordinarily content to teach, read a book, write poetry or go for walks in the country, he had presumed that this was how his life would be forever. Marriage was for others. He had nothing against marriage or indeed women, but the two had never seemed to fit together and make the ultimate sense that seemed obvious to so many of his acquaintances, and indeed, to the rest of the world. His attitude was only hardened by his experience; believing it was hard enough leaving his parents behind, let alone a wife, and possibly children too, as many of his army colleagues had done. How could they bear to be parted?

And so at 25, Howard was happily single; at least for the foreseeable future.

In fact he'd never even kissed a girl; this is if he didn't count the girls who'd fallen for the uniform a few months earlier: and that wasn't love, or at least he hoped it wasn't.

Howard was, on first impressions, *old before his time*, and the world outside he kept at a safe arm's distance. Most young men were thrilled at the prospect of leaving home: Howard was more thrilled to have returned there after completing his training in 1912. Knowledge was the great focus for him and from a young age he had fed hungrily on the arts. Books were his great weakness, or rather, as he constantly reminded himself, his strength, and with the dawn of the new century came a whole new wave of bright, new and optimistic new writers, poets and painters. And then, when all seemed so hopeful, and undeniably possible, from nowhere came this war. Although by then his grasp was strong and undeniable. He had 'found himself' through the paintings and sculptures of the artists and in the words of the writers and during the worst of his depression those words and images were among the few things that had helped to retain his sanity.

Of course there was always his family. Although they had, in his eyes, stepped back from him since he returned from the war. They had lost that power over him as Howard had become his own man by going off to fight, and he felt that the shock of nearly losing him distanced him from them by being the one too *dangerous* to love. Even his mother, who believed that Howard could do no wrong admitted, 'It's hard to see you and hug you without imagining you dead. The thought terrified me and still does and I don't know if I can trust you again".

This confession had brought Howard to his knees, yet he would be eternally grateful to his mother for an insight he was incapable of making without her forthright honesty. It served as the first of many steps to bring Howard out of his many *shells*: firstly the shell that was his desire for knowledge and now another shell to add to the list, the mysterious one, even to himself - that of his depression.

Before Ypres his life was fine. He'd worked hard, got his teaching certificate and then came the perfect job at the local school. He had his family, his books, nature and a job he loved; and then Ypres and the mortar blast.

During his convalescence that summer this became the subject he would mostly obsess about. He would walk it with him around the hills, he'd journal it and talk it over with Dr Manning or whoever would listen. So many things in his life seemed to be at odds with each other now, whereas before there was order and control. Was he to believe that this was all part of growing up, becoming more experienced? 'Is it me or is it the rest of the world that's mad?'

The search for self-understanding led him to a friendship that he would value and respect for the rest of his life. At his mother's suggestion; who firmly believed that his soul, as well as his state of mind, was in need of reparation, he sought the guidance of the local Methodist minister, a man in his early thirties, newly arrived in Derbyshire.

# JOURNAL: MAY 1915

Today I met with Tom again at the vicarage. Mother made the initial suggestion and I, with some apprehension agreed. We were already acquainted as the family regularly attends chapel, so this made it all a little easier.

Tom, who is 33, eight years my senior, shares many of my interests, but specifically nature and literature. He studied Theology and Contemporary Writers at Oxford and took on his first parish in Luton, Bedfordshire, seven years ago. Since then he has travelled abroad, working first in South Africa then briefly in China with the Methodist Missionary Society. During the last year he offered his services to the armed forces where he has been field chaplain in both France and Belgium. He is married with one small daughter, Emily, who is soon to be eight. His wife Margaret, a beautiful, but sadly, frail woman, is the main reason he came to Derbyshire. Four months ago she was diagnosed with tuberculosis, whereupon Tom immediately applied for a post where his wife's condition might in time, improve.

It seems we are all surrounded by, or linked to, death at this time. And whilst discussing this topic Tom said something that I at first thought strange, but then on second hearing, became a deeply moving thought. He said he believes that there has to be a very good reason for war and disease to enter our lives, and that is to remind all mankind of their ultimate duty to one another - that being the long forgotten act of compassion (he adds disease to note not only his wife's TB, but also the influenza epidemic that has claimed so many lives, both here at home and on the battlefield).

I stared back at him with uncertainty, trying to fully understand his statement.

"Compassion? Helping the sick, the needy, the dying?"

To which he replied, "Yes, but now we need to take it further, make it all embracing and meaningful. Compassion now must mean 'to suffer with' and 'feel their pain', and really feel it. Live it with them and by doing so, help to alleviate it."

This simple, but passionate statement stunned me.

"You mean, not only carry our own cross, but to also help other's with theirs? Like Simon did for Jesus?"

"Yes, and more besides. Remember Corinthians1, chapter 15, verse 55 - Oh death where is your sting? Oh grave where is thy victory?"

"And by having faith and sharing it…"

"Yes, but think again and more deeply: Think of the thousands who have died and the thousands more this war seems likely to claim. Should we believe them all guilty of some crime to be butchered in this way? Or should we believe something more meaningful is happening in order for these young men on both sides to be chosen for such a fruitless end? All things in life revolve around cause and effect, and sometimes the two don't necessarily add up, but if we give them time, even this war might eventually make sense."

"A new order… a new plan…?"

"Yes, but based on the original statement made by Christ when he said, 'For all those who believe in me, they need not die, but live with me forever in heaven."

"Eternal life… we are born, we live we die, and are born again… And again… And again… Reincarnation."

"Of course, but as we live, remember compassion. I see a time when everyone in this country, this continent, will have lost someone dear or at least will know someone who has lost someone dear. If we have the faith to watch this madness knowing all the while that God is purely sane, and offers a different way of understanding all this, then it's a small step to believe that death really has no sting. That this and other lifetimes, before and after this one, may teach us something grander than being shot to death at 18. This time our experience has been painful, next time, hopefully it will be better. And by believing that we have no control over such things allows us to join up and risk dying: in essence, to freely give all and be rewarded by getting it all back - and maybe more."

"But isn't this just a way of justifying death and suffering? Why can't we simply have a good life and leave it at that?"

"With no ups and downs, no rounded experience, no formation of character? I don't think so. What are the heights of passion without also experiencing the depths of despair?"

"And it is faith, pure and simple that allows this process? Faith: the belief in something we may never prove…"

"Quite, but cross over the road and live in that faith and see how good life can be. Howard, who or what is God to you? Is he a mischievous old man with a grey beard or what?"

"Certainly not..."

"It's okay, I'm only joking."

"Okay, all right… No, he's ageless, faceless and timeless. A blade of grass. A new born baby. A smile… He's us… He's nature… He's all things. In fact I think *he* is probably a *she.* For she is, and has, such beauty, such innocence, such a bountiful being, such creativity. It seems we men only want to kill each other, and in doing so, wreak havoc on all that surrounds us. There is much we need to learn from women…"

At that moment Margaret broke up the discussion by

entering the study with a tray laden with tea and cakes.

"Indeed Howard. Women think of everything. What would we do without them?"

At which he turned to his wife and tentatively smiled, knowing perhaps that in the not-too-distant future his own faith would be put to the ultimate test.

# TAKING STOCK

That night Howard lay in bed pondering over the afternoon's conversation with Tom. He finally concluded, after some considerable heart searching, that Tom might just be the person responsible for bringing out the finer things in him.

Hadn't he returned from the vicarage refreshed, invigorated, and above all, more excited about the prospects that life had to offer? It appeared to Howard that Tom could be indefinitely capable of unlocking his dark and fearful side. And while some of what Tom had said was new and peculiar to him, especially coming from his local minister, it wasn't however, in any way alien to him. It was as if he'd been waiting for this someone to appear and encourage him in a new way of thinking and seeing things. He had felt more alive around Tom; more hopeful. And while Howard hoped that Dr Manning might indeed continue to probe and provoke his inner blockage and depression, he felt that in Tom, he might gain something very tangible and important - a friend. He thanked God for putting Tom into his life and unlocking a part of himself he had only before glimpsed from a distance. There would be both knowledge and friendship in this new relationship he'd made.

# JOURNAL: MAY 1915

Tom has opened my mind to so much. It's as if I'm considering things on a national level, and then the next day, an international level. His years of travel have served him well with what he is now forced to cope with: a nation's grief. By comparison, my study in, and teaching of, English Literature, has left me sadly lacking in the affairs of nations and men.

Only last year I was happy in my own little world of Shakespeare and Milton, where everything made perfect sense, when there was harmony without discord. There was soccer, cricket and cream teas, boat trips on the river, parasols and boaters, bank holidays and day trips, and summers in Skegness and Mablethorpe. This last year has seen the end of all this. Life will not be the same again, ever. Never again will people look at themselves and each other, with the same joy and innocence. As Tom said, 'Soon everyone will be touched in one way or another by this war'. And as a result I see us limping, blinking, licking our wounds, and no matter how long we cry and mourn, we will never regain that innocence: forever our minds will be filled with the unnatural horrors of this war. There will be pieces missing, or at best, permanently frozen. Those of us who have survived will dream forever of those who perished around us. We will wake screaming, years hence, believing we are back there amid the frantic madness, the blasts, bright flashes and the frightened white eyes. Families will say grace and add another line to save them more empty places at the dinner table. There is hysteria over small, brown, government envelopes. And because we are all touched, there is no-one to blame, although we try. And when all else fails, we blame God. And in doing so, feel ashamed to be angry, lonely, lost and unloved. The cycle seems eternal. The circle is indeed viscous.

I ask Tom how he keeps it up, and he says it can't harm you if you keep loving it and embracing it with all you have. He says that if we all stop loving because our hearts are broken, we might just as well give up now -

'This is only part of the plan. Don't give up, we're not half way there yet'.

I have to believe sometimes that there is more than a bit of madness in faith: just as there has to be a speck of love somewhere in all this hate, fear and sadness.

# JOURNAL: MAY 24<sup>TH</sup> 1915.

I find the duality of life such a burden. The chat Tom and I had the other day filled me with such hope, maybe too much. Since then I have been filled with the thought of death: my brush with it, my sights of it, the smell and taste of it. And while I haven't committed much of my thoughts on the subjects of war and death, to my journal, I feel honour-bound to at least acknowledge them in a more… thoughtful and constructive way. Being so close as I was to death has, since my discussions with Tom, reminded me about my life and the plans I should have: what is it I want to achieve?

Before Ypres, it seems my life was barely half-full; I see that clearly now. And yet I believed it to be full. Tom, in his openness, has shown me, I am not as worldly as I would like to believe. Today I feel at odds with the world; fearful of what it might have in store and yet, at the same time, excited beyond words at what might be my true potential and direction. And while the human race is cursed by having to live life *in duality*, I concede that without nearly dying I would not have the same view on life. And there seems no way around the problem as I see it, that without one side, I may not have the other. So I am grateful to the one that led me to the other; realising though, that when I now feel the fall into despair, it is much greater, but conversely, when there is despair, its opposite is now the mountaintop of joy. (I laugh when I consider my previous extremes of either a good day or a bad day at work).

And so it has been death that I have been concerned with lately: and never again an ordinary death through accident or disease, now that I have tasted the 'Hero's Death'. And yet I wonder, what is more heroic, to die for one's country, or for one's beliefs?

That's maybe where my sense of exaltation comes from. It has to be belief; or maybe the both can be combined in a *Perfect hero's death,* that satisfies both dictates. I have to say, however, that this last death, seems for me, unlikely.

I am immediately mindful of the boys that died, while I lived. I know my guilt is foolish and futile, but I wonder, were they conscious of what happened? Were they positioned in such a way as to shield me if a shell did land close by? And, did they believe their young lives ultimately led them to a sudden and violent end on a piece of anonymous, nondescript, war-ravaged, stinking, strip of nowhere?

'Don't promise me wings, I will only disappoint you.'

There is so much I have to understand, and so much I still have to go through. If my appendix burst tomorrow, and I died, I would only think what a pointless waste my life had been. I could find little reason or sense in it all: a means to a shallow end. But then again, if I died a hero's death tomorrow, then everything's been so much more worthwhile. And while I sense I am being far too dramatic about it all, I have to say again, for the umpteenth time, *Why was I spared and for what reason.* And when I ask the question the possibilities seem endless and my thirst for life is boundless, ever since I first tasted death.

As if it wasn't enough to be on a constant see-saw of emotional extremes, today I met the most beautiful, sensitive, and thoroughly wholesome woman in creation! Where do I start?

She is 18, nearly 19, and comes from Dover. Her parents, from a well to do banking family, considered her safer in the Midlands, living with an aunt during weekends and holidays, while studying at Nottingham

College during the week. Her term starts in two weeks, and she is studying English and Drama, with a view to teaching. She is tall, about 5feet 8inches, with long dark hair. Physically, although she was dressed in a most unflattering Macintosh, she appears slim and willowy with delightfully trim ankles.

The downpour not only necessitated her wearing the unsightly garment, but also brought us to the same place of temporary shelter. Robin's Teashop on the High Street, which is where I took shelter from the rain, and other than the war, rain has been the only other consistent feature of the year so far. Not surprisingly, the teashop was full to overflowing. I was about to turn and leave when a hand shot up from a table in the corner, accompanied by a "Cooee", that I recognised straight away as the unmistakable chimes of Flora Gardner, the drama teacher at school.

Flora, whose beauty is matched only by the attentiveness of her husband, is a genuine, wild one. Her beauty is radiant, her talent spontaneous, her nature... untamed. So much so, that while I enjoy her conversation and company I feel somewhat vulnerable in an odd sort of way when I'm with her, that I have to wonder how her husband copes with her.

So I was relieved when I saw she was with somebody else and gladly accepted the invitation to share the table. In due course, I was introduced to her niece, Miss Angela Newbold, together with the immediate details of her appearance in Derbyshire. She, Angela, sat quietly as we discussed her. Occasioally she glanced up from her tea and pastry and smiled politely, with a pair of the bluest eyes I've ever seen. The contrast of the egg-shell like skin, the eyes and the hair, is disquieting.

# MAY 29<sup>TH</sup>, 1915.

"Howard, good see you again. Come in, sit down."

This time Howard was more attuned to the relationship.

"Thank you doctor. And yes I'm glad to be here… Any news of Ernest?"

Dr Manning momentarily looked away.

Howard bit his tongue, regretting the possible intrusion.

"No, no, nothing recently… Sure to have something soon, though."

"And Mrs Manning?"

"She's fine, keeping busy, you know…"

Howard knew only too well, and nodded in agreement.

"Now then, let's make a start… Howard, I want you to describe what it is you actually feel right now."

Dr Manning had been standing by the filing cabinet studying Howard's notes and occasionally glancing out the window. Howard waited until he took his seat, file in hand.

"Well doctor, I find it hard to actually describe how I truly feel."

"Mmm, and why is that do you think?"

Oh I don't know…" Howard shook his head. "It's as if the feeling, whatever it is, changes on a regular basis, usually depending on my surroundings."

"Now that's interesting. So you feel different here than you do at home?"

"Yes, certainly."

"Do you feel better or worse here?"

"I suppose in the end, it appears a question of better or worse, but I don't see it as simple as that."

"Simple?"

"Yes, simple. I mean, there's so much less to

consider here isn't there?"

"If you mean people's feelings, yes."

"I mean people's feelings and more…"

"Which is…?

"Knowledge."

"You mean, for example, if I say shell shock or you say depression, there is not the same need to explain one's self?"

"That's a good way of putting it. Thank you."

"Which saves you from baring your soul. But what else is it Howard?"

"I don't like to talk about it too much. It just causes them so much pain."

"So you keep quiet in order not to upset your parents?"

"Sometimes I do… and sometimes I go for walks."

"And who gets upset when you go for a walk?"

"That's an interesting question."

"Why so?"

"Because I hadn't looked at it that way before."

"What way, Howard… What hadn't you seen?"

Howard was suddenly silent and felt small and helpless. Not that this was Dr Manning's intention, more the 'talking cure'. Howard gazed up from his hunched body, staring blindly through Manning.

"There are times when I see too much." Howard's voice was trembling.

"Too much of what, Howard?"

"Too much of everything, doctor."

"Tell me one thing you've seen too much of?"

"Empty seats, doctor… empty seats."

"And where do you see these empty seats?"

"Everywhere doctor… everywhere…"

"So this is a metaphoric answer, Howard?"

"Yes and no."

"Help me, Howard, will you?"

Howard, still staring up through his glassy eyes, nodded.

"Help me by closing your eyes for a minute."

Howard continued to stare.

"Just for a minute, close your eyes."

Manning's voice rose a couple of decibels and Howard's eyes closed slowly.

"What do you see when you close your eyes, Howard?"

There was no answer, but for a tear that ran down is face.

"Where do you go to when you close your eyes, Howard?"

Slowly Howard spoke. "It's difficult, doctor, so very hard."

"And that's all right, Howard. Remember that you're safe, and in my office at Nottingham General Hospital."

Howard remained silent.

"Where would you have to be to feel safe, Howard?"

There was still no answer, and then… "Dead… dead." Howard began to shout and shake his head about. "Dead, dead. I'd have to be dead to be safe."

Manning looked concerned. What should he do next? He wished he was more experienced. And yet experience was exactly what was staring him in the face.

"What would being dead solve, Howard?"

Howard began breathing heavily, and was visibly shaking.

"What would it solve?" Manning's voice was sterner this time, but he omitted the reference to death. He wondered if the word alone terrified Howard.

"It would make me the same as the rest." Howard choked.

"The same as who, Howard? Who are you referring to?"

Howard began to say something, but subsided into fits of tears. He cried for three or four minutes, during which time, Manning encouraged the process.

"It's all right to cry Howard. It's healthy and cleansing."

Eventually he stopped crying and once again regained his composure enough to speak.

"When was the last time you cried, Howard?"

"Oh, I can't remember... Maybe months ago... maybe years."

"And how does it feel?"

At this, Howard raised his head, and opening his eyes replied...

"It feels good, doctor. I haven't cried like this ever."

"And can you tell me where you were in your mind's eye?"

Something close to a smile spread across Howard's face. It was a smile of remembrance as well as sadness.

"I was at school, doctor... at school. All those empty desks... those missing children."

"But they'd left school, Howard, they were grown."

"Not in my eyes. They'll be forever children in here." Howard said, pointing to his head. "And there's a part of me that wants to be with them."

"I can understand that. You feel responsible... Even..."

Manning couldn't finish his sentence.

"Responsible? Me? Oh no, not responsible. How could I be, I let them die."

"...Guilty."

Manning completed his sentence.

"But I should have gone with them."

"It's hard to be a survivor, isn't it, Howard?"

"Is this all there is...?"

"Oh no, Howard, there's much more. You've just started the process, I assure you it gets better."

"I hope so… I certainly hope so."

# JOURNAL: MAY 29<sup>TH</sup>, 1915.

For a second this afternoon I thought I was losing my mind. Dr Manning's questions tore right into my sadness and I had no defence. My head just got tighter and tighter until I thought it would implode. Is this what the talking cure is about? Do I sit and go back in time to that blinding flash that left me dead, but still ticking?

I have many questions, too many. But will their answers take away this feeling, this sickness? I fear that nothing will take the memory away - It lives just as all my past does in the recesses of my mind. Will the doctor reach in and merely take it out for me? I believe not. Then where will it go? I neither want nor need it, but there is this dreadful pleasure I get from reliving its torment. It comes to mind anytime it pleases, day or night, awake or asleep. In a grotesque way it is my guilty reminder that I am still alive and I have the feeling it may go on forever.

The coldness goes on too. Sometimes I go completely rigid for no conscious reason. At night I lie on my back and do my best to sleep - this is the hardest time. It is the night when the memories are most vivid and the pictures are once again fed into the projector, just to make sure I have not forgotten anything.

# JOURNAL: MAY, 1915.

They say that we British are obsessed with the weather and that is all we can talk about. I can only agree with this. But there is more to it than that: a much deeper relationship that other nations might fail to appreciate. Unlike many other countries we fully experience all four seasons and being a country where farming plays an important part in both our working life and national economy, it follows that our welfare, to a degree, is dependent on those seasons. Also, we are an island - a sea-faring nation forever at the mercy of the weather.

From these shores we have sailed for discovery and have colonised a large majority of the 'new world'. Also, don't forget that we have put to sea on many occasions to defend this country of ours. Folklore and tradition therefore dictate that we are governed by the weather; it is in our blood. We feel each light breeze and every cloud that crosses the sun. And we are both fearful and respectful of a climate that can allow us summer days in October as well as snow in June: the crux being the consistency of the inconsistency, together with the nagging desire to carry an umbrella on a hot August day, just in case. And as a people we have become somewhat like our weather; changeable and inconsistent: ask our friends; ask our enemies. And don't believe in stereotypes.

Ever since that night at Ypres my life has changed considerably. Like the weather I have become more inconsistent and fearful of 'what would've happened if...'

Sleep is now something I no longer rely on occurring during the normally accepted hours as I now have a new 'inner alarm' that respects little that I have been previously used to. For example, last night I retired at 11pm to write my journal in bed, with "lights out" at about 11.30. Without any reluctance I drifted off into a deep sleep; I dreamed, then woke with the feeling that I had had a good night's sleep. Glancing at the clock I saw that it was 2.45am. Immediately I panicked at feeling one thing and seeing another. And with the panic comes the desire to return to sleep (as it is not normal for me to rise at 2.45am), although two minutes before I had felt rested and refreshed after what I thought was a good night's sleep. Again I sleep, but I awake many more times before the alarm goes off at the normal time of 8am; when I feel worse than I did at 2.45. Both doctors, Dr Manning and my local GP, say it is my depression, my melancholy. This I cannot doubt as my normal sleeping times have altered so drastically since the explosion. Both doctors reassure me that, in time, all will hopefully return to normal, but I have to be patient. I have learned not to be frustrated by this inconsistency. Moreover, I try to go along with it, which entails me living a totally revised schedule as I might get up and start my day at 4am and later alleviate my fatigue with a cat-nap in the middle of the afternoon, or straight after dinner.

Living this revised schedule has taught me to appreciate inconsistency. There are benefits to be gained from every change, conscious or not, and it is my task to find the silver lining in this dark sky in order to make the unacceptable, acceptable.

I now experience those dark hours more fully. I may feed hedgehogs bread and milk at 5am, and walk the hills at first light, encountering rabbits and foxes and occasionally, a badger or a family of deer. Experiencing life from a slightly different angle has me feeling closer to nature, but in turn brings back that sinking feeling again. And the longer this vicious cycle of memories and associations go on I realise that it is only me, within my life, and when I put it all together and acknowledge it, I have this desire to explore, understand and embrace. This is all part of me and part of the adventure.

If nothing else we British are always prepared to deal with our inconsistencies and are ready, at a moment's notice, to turn 180 degrees to attempt to comprehend the unexpected.

This morning I awoke at four and decided to remain conscious and not try to return to sleep. So I lay awake and thought for a while; to consider yesterday and wonder about today. I prayed for peace and I prayed for the safety and sanity of all mankind. I then got dressed, had a light breakfast and pulled my boots on to walk outside, and was welcomed by the dawn chorus. I walked in the half-light, through the familiar long grass and pathways of the valley. The air was chilly and fresh and the dew dripped like cool honey from what seemed like every plant, stalk of grass, from every branch and leaf on the trees. I walked by the river and breathed the light mist that hung by the banks. The sky was a perfect, cloudless blue, and as the sun rose it felt like the dawn of a new age, and not just another day. I felt invigorated and ran and fell about laughing in the long grass, not caring what sight I might appear to be to any passer-by, and buried my face in that refreshing, green-smelling sea.

Summer was returning and all seemed brighter, richer, more optimistic; warmer. For once, Ypres seemed a little more distant than usual, and this place, my birthplace, was beginning to feel like home again. That emptiness in my stomach was fading, my head felt clearer and my eyes were really seeing again, and not just drifting...

Slowly I rose to my knees and looking to the sky I smiled. "Thank you... thank you... thank you... thank you...", ran around in my head and exited finally from my mouth as a passionate cry of "Let this be the first of better days", as I got to my feet, brushing the dew from my clothes. Something inside is returning to my life after weeks of inactivity. I will be whole again!

# JUNE 5$^{TH}$, 1915.

Howard arrived for his third, weekly appointment with Dr Manning. He'd been feeling better of late and was anxious to discuss what he considered to be his first flavour of recovery.

"So, how have you been feeling, Howard?"

"Better doctor, a little better I think."

"Good. Any particular reason?"

"Oh, I don't know really. Maybe Spring is in the air."

"Spring's been in the air a while now, Howard."

"But maybe not in my air, doctor."

"Very good, Howard. I like that... like it a lot... an interesting thought."

"Yes it is, isn't it."

Howard froze for a second, then smiled. Manning saw this.

"How do you *feel* Spring, Howard?"

Howard thought for a moment.

"I think it's intuitive, isn't it?"

"Intuitive... but for everyone?"

"Oh yes, for everyone."

"And what about the people in the cities? I mean, it's fine for you out there in the country, but what about the rest of us, shrouded in smog and smoke...?"

"Mmm... yes..."

Howard looked puzzled for a moment and then continued.

"But don't the seeds and bulbs lie dormant underground, waiting for the signal of Spring?"

"Well, if you put it like that, yes, I suppose they do."

Both men stared into thought. Manning spoke first.

"Sounds like one of those poems you write... waiting for the signal of Spring..."

Again they fell silent.

"And do the dead feel Spring?"

Howard's voice was barely a whisper.

"Sorry Howard, what did you say?"

Howard was miles away: distracted, yet attentive to some inner music. Without thinking he repeated the words, this time a little louder than before.

"And do the dead feel Spring?"

Manning felt a sudden desire to turn the subject around to provoke a positive response.

"You have a gift, Howard."

"I do? And what is that doctor?"

"The gift of words."

"Oh, I'm not sure about that... Well, I am a teacher I suppose..."

"But it's more than that, surely?"

Howard thought, nibbling at a fingernail.

"Yes, you're right of course."

"And what is it that you write?"
"Oh nothing really, just poems."

"Just poems? Don't say that to Mr Lawrence will you now."

They both smiled.

"And where are these poems?"

"In my head mostly."

"You don't write them down? Don't you forget them?"

"Some I write down... when they're ready, of course. But the others just roll around in there... gathering meaning... waiting..."

Howard stopped in mid-sentence. He appeared frightened, maybe a little threatened, almost as if he was aware that he was giving away a precious secret. While for Manning, he hadn't gone far enough.

"And what is it they're waiting for, Howard? These poems, what do they need?"

Howard looked away. It was time for Manning to do some leading.

"Sometimes Howard, it's simply a case of finding the right medium to unleash our pain. Holding on to our pain only stagnates that soil inside us. And without pain, there can be no growth. For you it's harnessing those words, moulding them into something... something..."

Manning hesitated, hoping Howard would supply his own end to the sentence.

"... Pure, something pure."

"Absolutely. Something pure. But as pure as what?"

Howard thought for a minute.

"I'm not sure..." He thought again. "But it could be that first sense of Spring. The purity of birth, of re-birth, the greenness, the freshness. Renewed energy, the thrusting of small, green fingers... down into the earth..."

Manning sat gently smiling, relishing the wordy outburst.

"It's life isn't it, doctor?"

Manning nodded.

"But do the dead feel Spring?"

"I think they must Howard."

"But how...?"

"Maybe through us... The living."

Howard's eyes tightened, questioning.

"Do you really think so?"

Manning nodded again.

"I'm not so sure..."

"Then maybe it's not really Spring after all, Howard."

# JOURNAL: JUNE 5<sup>TH</sup>, 1915.

## Poem: And Do the Dead Feel Spring?

And do the dead feel spring,
and do their fingers tingle alive
as they touch the broken
and everlasting night?
And do their eyes tremble
and flicker in desperate attempts
to open the magic box of light?

And there is a heart there also,
but with no memory of warmth
that beats cold in its forgetfulness.

And the limbs still twisted,
with the ragged flesh
of wounds too old to heal.

And now as the season's blur
I wonder…
Do the dead feel spring?
… as their tears fill my eyes.

# JOURNAL: JUNE 19<sup>TH</sup>, 1915.

When she and I met at the teashop those few weeks ago my immediate response was of joy. For the first time in my life I felt I could be complete, although before then I had no concern as to feeling incomplete. I had parents, good friends and the job of my choice and then, out of the blue came Angela.

In a way she scared me, and though I know why, I wish it had been different. For when I thought of us together, all I could see was Margaret and Tom's slow decline. And so marriage became another definition of death to me. All this I know sounds perverse and serves, if nothing else, as a disturbing reflection of my present state of mind. A subject I intend to take up with Dr Manning at my next appointment.

# JOURNAL: THE MEMORIAL, JUNE 23$^{RD}$, 1915.

Oh dear me. What a day. And yet it seems too easy and somewhat predictable to describe such a day thus. Although, what is a journal, if not a subjective record of events? And before even the day broke there were the dreams. And sleep. Sleep can be such a cruel illusion. Last night I dreamt two dreams, simultaneously. First I dreamt of the beautifully, rugged Peak District that surrounds our village, while intermittently, I was visited by the antithesis of this natural beauty, the battlefield, with its blackened and sinister, skeletal trees and oceans of cloying mud. And even as the alarm sounded its shrill call for me to return to the day, I continued this battle of memories, in an effort to remain high up on a rocky outcrop, gulping down gallons of pure, country air. I didn't want today, neither did I want yesterday. I wanted that time of innocence, before all of this pain landed in my life. And I would have done anything to restore it.

Since the explosion at Ypres I have regularly had these deep, gut-feelings of abhorrence upon waking. Dr Manning suggests quite correctly, that it is a morbid reluctance toward my own life. And today of all days this observation could not be more accurate as my singular loathing at exchanging innocence for terror suggests.

Each night when I finally sleep, everything I dream of is tinged with the knowledge that I can only escape this depression temporarily. That wherever I flee or whoever I am, I will only ultimately return to this frightful, meandering existence. There are good days and there are bad, but they all start out the same: with me attempting to deny who and what I am, and what

I've become. And some of this fear is because I don't really know who or what I am. And while it is nothing short of blasphemy, I feel like what I imagine Christ felt, just before his crucifixion, asking to have the cup taken from me. And some mornings the fear is so strong I feel almost like ending it all. I don't want it; I can't stand it; and yet I can't avoid it either. And I beg for salvation.

And here I find myself today, in a strangling web of confusion; not wanting to be me; not wanting to be any of the me's that I inhabit. Feeling guilty about being me and feeling worse for them being gone, and knowing I am powerless about doing anything about the situation. Thank god Tom and Angela are accompanying me. This was something I didn't want to do alone.

My head was *tight* as I wrestled with my thoughts. Eyes tight-shut, hoping for more than I dared. The air in my room smelt of sweet pipe tobacco, and slowly I surfaced. Or did I descend?

At 7.30 I dressed quietly and went for my morning walk. There was a mist on the Peaks and the air was wet, but not cold. I headed for a small, grassy hill that recently I have adopted as my own, about a mile or so from home. The words of the Hymn "There is a green hill far away..." entered my head, and I felt wretched for wanting Him to relieve me of my burden, my fears, maybe even my life. Today is not for me, or even about me. It is for them, "The Fallen Heroes", as the newspapers describe them, to a readership desperate for tales of heroism. If only they knew the truth. There are no heroes out there, only terrified young men doing what they want to believe is right and knowing all the time that there must be a better way.

It's strange, but before the explosion fear was something irrelevant. It was something we would talk about after a night's recon, but never during, and even then in a decidedly detached manner. And even seconds before that fateful blast I can still see those faces alive with adventure, believing that later that night we would all sit down together to exchange our various points of view on the evening's activities over a nice, sweet cup of tea. Never once did we contemplate or discuss death. War was a risky venture, but never a terminal one. We were amongst friends, morale was high, and while all around us the casualties stared, not once did we consider our own mortality. How real can death be to a group of boys and young men who, a matter of a few weeks earlier, had been bank clerks, farm hands, miners, college students and schoolteachers? And would we have joined up so enthusiastically if those newspapers had reported the war with a little more honesty? Probably so, as no-one can describe adequately what war is like. It is like talking about death to a young man: it's something beyond his comprehension.

I sat on my hill wondering as all of these thoughts washed around and through me. I was desperate for words, as I have been invited by the families to give a brief elegy; and there I sat, schoolmaster and writer, bereft of ideas. Silently I prayed that the right words would indeed come to me. I returned home briskly, eyes fixed on the path ahead.

{I have re-read what I have written and I feel so ashamed when I spoke of feeling alone. How could I feel alone in a village of some 800 souls, most of whom I have known all my life!! The ugliness of fear! The illusion of sleep!

The chapel will be packed with friends and acquaintances and familiar faces. How could I have been so selfish?}

A group of about fifteen mourners assembled at our house, including Angela. At 10.30, after fitful chatter and a glass of father's sherry we embarked on the half-mile walk to the chapel; clutching hymn books, wreaths and wild flowers, but most of all, each other. We huddled, linked arms and shuffled slowly to the old, gray-stone, village chapel: a building that has been no stranger to grief during its 221 year history. And it is said that we learn from our experience!

The familiar strains of hymns and marching tunes, played by our local colliery band, filled the quiet morning air as we approached the chapel, and once again I found myself singing "There is a green hill far away…", silently to myself. The chapel was packed with mourners lining the walls and aisles. The chapel bells rang a reverential eleven times after which Tom began the service with the hymn "Oh God our help in ages past…" We all did our best, amid tears and the blowing of noses.

Needless to say, there were no coffins here. The remains of the boys we mourned today lie, as Rupert Brooke prophetically wrote, "In a corner of a foreign field that is forever England". And it was with these lines that I began my elegy.

"This is the first and finest verse of Rupert Brooke's poem, Soldier. And I have to wonder if he, who lies at peace in his own foreign field, would describe himself solely as a soldier. I think not. In any case, no more than the seven young men we have come here to remember today. My own feelings on this saddest of days prevents me from claiming a rank, as I believe, regardless of race, creed or nationality, that we are first and foremost, children of God. And as a child of God I come here today not to question the acts of our Father, but to remind us all that we are here to play a part in something we have little knowledge of.

I have no words of explanation, as to why these young men, like the thousands of others, have been chosen to die: though I wish I could say something to, in some way, lighten our hearts. So what is it that we can share together that will convince us that these young lives were not lived in vain or sacrificed lightly?

As most of you know, I was with these young men when they perished, and if it wasn't for my fortunate proximity, I too would be mourned here today. As most of you will also know, I taught these young men, at one time or another, at St Thomas', and therefore I too have my cross to bear, so to speak. My recovery thus far, both physical and mental, has been made possible by two men, who a few weeks ago were unknown to me. The first of these is Dr Manning at the Nottingham General Hospital, and second is our own good friend and minister, the Reverend Tom Davis. Both these fine men are helping me sort out my many, tangled emotions by reminding me that life, in essence, is very simple, and above all we experience it together, and not in isolation. And if anyone is in doubt about this, please look around and remind yourselves of the strength and support that surrounds each of us.

We are a mining community and are therefore no strangers to disaster, and it seems in a peculiar way, almost in a biblical sense, that when one of our number suffers, we all suffer, and as a result we find the strength to continue. This morning as I walked the moors, thinking about what I might say to make our grief, not simply disappear, but to at least try to ease the pain of it, I was forced to acknowledge my limitations. There is nothing I can say, there is nothing I can do. And while it is us, the living, who are left with this desperate feeling we call grief, today I would ask you all to consider the dead. They had their fears, mostly unspoken, but acknowledged none-the-less with a glance or a wink of the eye. But for them the terror and madness of war was tempered by their unquestioning loyalty to each other and a silent pledge to the cause of victory. And while we shake our heads and mourn the passing of their youth we must also respect their sacrifice. To die for something they believed in was, in truth, not duty or waste, but honour. And while today we may not want to hear it justified as such, they have surely bought our freedom with their blood, as have the countless thousands across our small country. I, like all of us here today want peace, but not at any price. And as we offer our own silent prayers to the Almighty, we might also ask Him to act on humanity's behalf by guiding those, in all governments involved, to bring this war to an amicable close.

As most of you know, I am considered by some to be something of a poet. And during these past weeks I have had a line in my head that kept returning to me time and time again. Eventually, after a particularly emotional session with Dr Manning the rest of the poem magically appeared. Writing poetry is a peculiar discipline and at times it does seem that they in some way, write themselves. The line I speak of is "as their tears fill my eyes", and I would like to read the completed poem for you today. Above all it is a hopeful poem, that acknowledges life, death and suffering through the question, "and do the dead feel Spring?" And my hope is that we will, when the sadness of our loss subsides, again feel the familiar breath of Spring in our lives. And by acknowledging our loss, we may again fully embrace our lives and the lives of those around us, forever mindful of the great sacrifice that has brought us together today."

> And do the dead feel spring,
> and do their fingers tingle alive
> as they touch the broken
> and everlasting night?

> And do their eyes tremble
> and flicker in desperate attempts
> to open the magic box of light?
>
> And there is a heart there also,
> but with no memory of warmth
> that beats cold in its forgetfulness.
>
> And the limbs still twisted,
> with the ragged flesh
> of wounds too old to heal.
>
> And now as the season's blur
> I wonder…
> Do the dead feel spring?
> … as their tears fill my eyes.

With the poem over, and with the last verse ringing in my ears and around my head, I looked out into the congregation, wondering how I should end my elegy. My mouth began something that my brain could not contemplate. I breathed deeply, staring up at the ceiling and ended up self-consciously bowing, not that I was expecting any response to my tribute, but more in homage to our collective loss. I walked back to my seat and realised that their tears would, to varying degrees, fill my eyes for the rest of my life.

# A CHANGE OF ROLES: JULY, 1915.

As Howard sat reading after lunch, Tom arrived.

"Take me for a walk Howard please. You know all the best places."

Tom's eyes were fixed on the floor. Howard said nothing, he just put his boots on and led the way.

"Where do you suggest we go, Howard?"

"Oh... somewhere quiet. I'll let you know when we get there."

It was a feeble attempt at humour, but Howard had sensed the worst and needed to steady himself.

"It's Margaret, isn't it?"

"Yes." Tom's head slowly nodded and then shook. "I woke up this morning and she'd gone during the night. She just lay there... white and cold, and staring."

Howard's mind went blank. And then, "Oh God."

"Oh God indeed. As if there wasn't enough death in the world."

The two men continued walking in silence. The dried grass crackled under their feet as they headed through the small copse and out onto the moor land. Tom was the first to speak.

"I envy you and your knowledge of this countryside. If our paths had never crossed I can't imagine what I might have done instead."

"I envy you your faith. Sometimes I see this place only as an escape."

"But we all need these places. And we certainly all need to escape at times."

"Even you...?"

"Especially me... especially today. I hope you think of me as a friend and not just your minister, because that's how I have come to you today, as a friend... a friend in need."

"Of course, Tom... of course, but..."

"But nothing. Believe me there are times when I have too much of the god in me and not enough of the man... And today it would be easy to hide behind the god and let the man off the hook."

Howard smiled at Tom's words and then gasped...

"Emily, Emily... what about Emily?"

"It's okay Howard, she's with the neighbours. She knows, but doesn't quite understand. We make a good pair..." Tom's words tailed off into silence as he stopped walking and slumped into the grass, brushing tears from his face. "If I don't understand, Howard, what am I going to tell her?"

For a moment Howard felt awkward and hoped the question was rhetorical as he wondered how he of all people could answer such a question. He'd met the little girl three or four times and said very little to her. What does one say to an eight year old girl? And then, in his mind's eye, he caught a glimpse of her, staring at him, pleading with her eyes.

"I think you tell her you love her. I think you pick her up and hug her a lot, and you tell her you love her."

Howard sank to his knees beside Tom and put his hand on his shoulder.

"But she and I... It's difficult. There's always been Margaret... And what with all the travel... we're a bit like strangers... Sounds crazy, but I'm scared... scared of... her. Scared of what she thinks... of what she doesn't think." He sat there shaking his head.

Look, I know... I'm not very good at this sort of thing, but you're going to need help for a while. You have a child and a parish to look after. You need a break... time to yourself. I suggest I move into the vicarage for a while and we'll manage as best we can. What do you think of that?"

Howard was asking a lot of Tom to even listen to his suggestions, but he hoped he would accept, "this act of compassion", as Tom would say, in the spirit it was meant.

Tom blew his nose loudly. They helped each other to their feet.

"You're a wonderful person, Howard, a surprising and wonderful... friend. I don't know what to say... I don't know what to feel... He gives and takes away, He tests me and He confuses me... And just before he loses me I have to remind myself that I don't have to know everything... every reason for everything. Just knowing enough is usually too much. I'm a slow learner too, I need to follow more and lead less..."

"So let's make a start and see where it leads us."

# CHRISTMAS EVE, 1915.

Howard sat at the lounge window. It was early morning, 7:15. Half an hour ago he had lit the fire and now the room was gradually warming. The frost on the window still clung to the glass in places, in its haphazard yet perfect pattern. It was Christmas Eve. Outside and away into the distance yesterday's snow of six inches or more lay untouched, but for the footsteps up and down the front path.

He heard Tom coming downstairs and rose to greet him.

"Well, aren't you the early bird?"

"I know... couldn't sleep. Doesn't matter though, I'm used to that."

"So what's on the agenda today, Christmas Eve?"

"Well, for one, I have to deliver presents. To the family and Angela and Flora. There'll be lunch and dinner, which should see me through well into the night and then it's the midnight carol service with you at the church."

"Well, someone needs to have it all in order. Good for you."

"But what about you, Tom, you and Emily?"

Tom never burdened Howard with his problems, believing that Howard had enough of his own. While Howard sensed Tom's pain in missing Margaret, but felt awkward making reference to it too regularly.

He had watched Tom throw himself into his work since Margaret's death, and while they had shared some time together it had never turned out exactly the way Howard had hoped it might: considering their conversations prior to Margaret's death and in particular, their passionate exchange during their walk on the day she died.

To a complete stranger, Emily would have appeared

to be Howard's child. How quickly the routine had established itself and how accurately it reflected Tom's fears on the day Margaret died.

Howard had returned to work in September and he and Emily would set of for school at eight in the morning and return, hand in hand, in the evening, and look for all the world to be father and daughter.

Although Howard felt for Tom and his difficult situation, his main concern rapidly became Emily. She may call him 'Uncle Howard', but he knew, for all intents and purposes, he was fast becoming, dad. It was a situation he'd seen coming plainly enough, but he always believed Tom would eventually respond positively to his daughter and rise above his 'fear of fatherhood'. As it turned out, it was a case of Howard having to step into Tom's vacant boots and not, as he expected, simply to retreat and let Tom take over: In the end he had straight forwardly welcomed her with open arms. The situation wasn't without its difficulties, but Howard argued to himself that "the child must have someone, and I'm better than no-one. It is her father's problem not mine, and he will, I am sure, at some point rejoin her life more fully. Until then I'll do my best not to feel awkward or in any way misplaced in my care for this young girl."

"Oh, we'll be all right… We've lots to do."

"You always say that, Tom, but it's usually me who ends up doing it."

"I know, I know… Oh Howard, she's so young and there's so much to take in and understand…"

"But you have to start somewhere, Tom. Look, you know I love you both dearly and I won't let Emily become a problem to us. Yes she has got a lot to take in and understand, but she and I talk about it, even though it would come better from her father. But this little girl is absolutely innocent, but there are times I know she feels somehow guilty, responsible for all this. I'm sure she sees you as pushing her away, and she thinks she's done something wrong... It's all getting very confused up there, in her head. I do my best, but she needs you to tell her she's innocent... that there's nothing wrong."

"Oh Howard, you're so very good at this. God, we're talking about my daughter, but all I do is run away from her. Where's the sense in it? This is madness. Help me Howard, it's so hard for me to work it out."

"Look, let me take her with me today, as it's Christmas Eve and you're busy."

"Would you Howard, thank you. I know I've been terrible so far and..."

"Enough, enough. I know you try and I'm not standing in judgement, but she needs more of you... Your love, your understanding and your compassion. She needs it and she deserves it. The girl has lost her mother and in her mind she's losing her father as well."

"I know, I know..."

Don't you think she misses Margaret too? And I'm the one who takes her to her grave! You could be sharing this responsibly and creating a relationship, a future..."

"All right, Howard, all right. It's just so hard when you can't even sort out your own grief, let alone your daughter's as well. Look, I don't have to be back until eight tonight to prepare for the service. Let's make a day of it: We'll visit your family, then go into town; I still have things I need to buy, and then we can all go to Angela's for a while. Hopefully they'll all put up with me."

"Of course, of course."

"Thanks Howard, you're a good friend, probably better than I deserve. And you're right of course... I mean, I've had days when I thought I was the guest here, watching you and Emily, then you and Angela. You look so happy... so complete. And then I look at myself and I wonder how I can get my life back together again, like you're doing. Don't stop being yourself, my friend, and remember, you're setting a fine example for me. Thank you Howard, you're a real blessing."

"Thanks Tom... I do my best, but you know it works both ways. It's a delight living here with you and Emily, and while I feel terrible admitting it, it's kept me away from the family... That's another thing this war has ruined, my family and me. You know they treat me like an invalid, not their son. Their caring was so claustrophobic and I don't know what I'd have done if I hadn't suggested moving in here. At some point I'll have to heal that relationship, and do you know, at present I'm at a loss as to how to approach it. But like you, I'll know when the time is right. You see, we've all got our problems that we feel powerless over, but one day soon we'll wake up and the right plan of action will be there waiting for us. So I'll help with Emily and you do your best with my parents when we see them today. Okay?"

"Okay. Things are a little clearer now. When you have problems, big problems, you think you're the only one. Thanks for waking me from that illusion."

"Yes, but there'll always be problems, regardless. Big problems, small problems, life's all about problems, but in the solving of them we might find them to be blessings in disguise. But for now, I'm happy. I have you and Emily, a roof over my head, fit again for work, and now Angela. I consider myself, to say the least, fortunate. And it's time that's the great healer, ultimately, but you still have to work at it. It doesn't just happen... And I must tell you, once more, that it was with your help and kindness that I have managed to come this far. The talks we had that filled me with renewed hope, that bolstered my faith... Kept me going."

"Seems like the roles have been reversed, somewhat. I've also learned from you, you know. I've learned that being a minister changes nothing. I still have my cross to bear, you might say, as I am excluded nothing for wearing the collar. It's like never expecting the doctor to get sick: having the minister lose his faith. And in that, and more, you've been a blessing.

Together we'll get through it... we have to. So let's start by having a marvellous Christmas. Come on, let's get Emily up, have breakfast, build a snowman and start the ball rolling!

# JOURNAL: JANUARY 15<sup>TH</sup>, 1916 – ON ROUTE TO SULVA BAY, TURKEY.

This troopship is a colossal, empty beast. I could be Jonah, and this the whale. There is activity, but it is quiet and orderly, as there are still a few days before we arrive in Sulva Bay. Rows of empty, comfortable looking beds await occupation. Nurses busy themselves putting the last, finishing touches to starched sheets and pillow cases. The weather remains cold and seems likely to get colder as we head east. I walk the decks endlessly; thinking and smoking.

Little is known about this particular campaign as there has been a news "blackout" ever since its inception last February. It wasn't until Murdoch's (an Australian journalist I believe) letter to his prime minister became public property last September that the beginnings of the whole sad, bungled truth came to light. This however, is not a history lesson as the facts will no doubt be told in grander ways during the coming years by those with much more to lose than merely their lives. Suffice to say that Gallipoli and the Dardanelles, which was originally perceived as an easy victory to promote optimism among the allies, and to divert the public gaze from the stalemate in France, ended in much the same way as Ypres, Flanders and the Marne: trench warfare and stalemate.

Officers, politicians, the commander-in-chief and Mr Churchill have all lost that which is, I'm sure, more than life to those involved; namely their jobs and for some, a permanent loss of reputation.

I wonder what this place is like, this little pinprick on the map that few have even heard of? The story is reminiscent of the Greek siege of Troy, and in the approximate area as well. Although the Greeks, for their part, warred for ten years, while we have had enough in less than one.

Enough, enough... I have come to find... no, I have come to find nothing. I have come to merely 'be'. I have had enough of my own madness, I now wish to sink back into someone else's for a while. I am back in uniform, but I've traded in my officer's revolver for a red cross armband. Death, for some reason, is stalking me, but doesn't seem to want to take me. And now I find myself split evenly between the grief for those I have lost and the peculiar possibility of being immortal. I have to suggest this ridiculous latter feeling as a way, however futile, of balancing the losses.

And so, what else would a partially immortal fool do other than re-join the war effort? Both Tom and Dr Manning remain neutral as to my decision. I sat with them both and reasoned that I was headed in a direction not marked with death, but to somewhere where I might indeed *find myself again*, by confronting once more, my own mortality.

What I hope to find, I'm not sure of. It might be in a sentence or a few words, something I might see or feel; I don't know. All I do know is that I must be here, on this ship, to follow my reason, however clouded it might be.

I feel I must say a little bit more about this feeling of immortality. Yes, it does sound frivolous, but it also has a solid foundation, so let me explain.

Firstly I am reminded of Tom and my conversations of last year when we spoke on the subject of death. How hopeful we both were and, as it turned out, justified, thinking and believing in such a way, when it would have been easier to be bitter and fearful. Today I feel that death has surely lost its sting, as the fear of it is indeed the sting itself.

From what I believe and have read, and what I have

gleaned from Dr Manning and Tom, death is seen by many to be the "one bad apple in the barrel", the one thing we avoid as best we can. And yet, by adopting this attitude, it quickly becomes the one thing we are able to rely on; that we will all die one day, so to speak. Death takes a firmer grip on our morbid senses when, for example, there is a war in progress or, as in our history, a plague sweeps the land. The resultant in both cases is that we are led to anticipate our death, and for many, I believe it possible to talk ourselves into the belief that there is no alternative other than death; and we occupy ourselves in its anticipation. This was particularly true in the case of my family when, upon my return from Ypres, there reaction was decidedly anti-climactic, as they perceived my going to war was synonymous with dying. In short they anticipated my death, and were indeed preparing for the worst, even before I had finished my training in Nottingham.

And so, I returned with my shell shock and guilt only to be greeted with disbelief and an odd sense of disappointment. And now, as mother has admitted, I am too dangerous to love, and I imagine them today being little bothered by my returning to action, because they cannot mourn the same person twice! Those threads of our connection have been well and truly severed. This also underlines how difficult it is to know one's own mind, when we have been conditioned to consider everyone else's as well. And it is similarly difficult to live one's own life and to develop one's own expectations and values, without also having to consider those that have dominion over us. And the results can be (mentally) crippling, but it is only by severing these threads that we can taste that sense of immortality: a belief that allows us to admit truthfully to ourselves that we will, ultimately die one day, but that we don't have to go through all these morbid expectations on a regular basis. This I believe is living in fear, the fear of everything we could be enjoying and exploiting to its best possible outcome.

The road to this point of my reasoning has not been a particular pleasant one; but then I don't believe we're here to experience only the good things, and throw all those "bad apples" out as if they didn't exist. It is *how* we react to both good and bad that is important.

Today I really believe that I don't have to die in order to feel good about myself, and that in itself is a major step forward.

In a matter of hours we will be docking in Skyros, the last stop before Sulva Bay, and my mind goes back to last year and to the death of Rupert Brooke, aboard a hospital ship, not unlike the one I presently travel in. Today he is looked upon as a hero / poet, and also as a martyr to the cause. For me, he will remain a remarkable man solely for the reason that he captured, in one poem, the hopes and fears of a whole nation, at odds with itself in a war the likes of which no-one had previously witnessed. And why this is so remarkable is simply that he (appears) to have based his 1914 Poems on a short tour of duty in Belgium, where it is said, "… the full horror of war struck him for the first time". Later that year he started his training in Dorset with the Hood Battalion, and was finally shipped out in February 1915. On his way out to Gallipoli he died of blood poisoning, and was buried in Skyros. Subsequently, many of his friends and colleagues were annihilated during the first few weeks of action.

There is much I would share on the topic of Rupert Brooke, yet I'm sure I would be viewed as being speculative and probably rather morbid. And yet, I will say it, regardless. The reference to his friends and colleagues confirms for me his prescience, his confirmation that war has no victors, and whatever he'd witnessed in Belgium, took root and stayed with him to the end - and maybe even heralded his end. From all accounts he was forever the optimist, the outgoing one, ready at a moment's notice to experience all that was new and exciting. And yet his life had been peppered with sadness and loss. First the death of his father and finally, and this is most speculative, the failed romance and the loss of his child. When I add his other broken romances and the first taste of war to this already tormented soul, I feel the overriding sense of doom that oozes from his poetry. He was, much like me and countless others, impelled to serve and yet, terrified by what he innately knew would be the result. Yes, it was an adventure, but with very real consequences that not even he, with his boyish optimism, could either deny or avoid. And that also presumes that *the* Rupert Brooke was indeed optimistic and not depressed as might be judged from reading his overall works. And while suicide is a strong word, he wouldn't have been the first to use war as an almost certain way out of a life that had lost its fascination: Regardless, one is non-the-less left with the feeling that something very primal resounded deep down in this young man in Belgium and, without a doubt, broke his will, if not also, his heart.

The nature of his death is also interesting, if you believe in that sort of thing. Basically, he died as a result of a gnat bite, and not as he was probably expecting, in battle. It's almost as if his nerve gave way and his natural bodily resistance gave up on itself. And so he would die in a similar fashion to the way he lived, slightly on the outside of things, and buried alone on a rugged hillside on a small Greek island.

His dye had been cast, and though it was not wholly of his making he was tiring of being the symbol of eternal youth. What he had written had cast him up, to his eternal surprise, head and shoulders above the rest, and consequently into a role that would never be truly of his making: One wonders what would have happened if the war had never been?

It's hard not to compare myself with him, as I know we share the same terror and frustration, that I'm sure he felt. When we dock in Skyros I will, out of deference to the man, sit and wonder beside his grave and see if I can envision a better end for myself: Me the teacher who runs away to war at the drop of a hat! And what is it I wonder that life has in store for me. Me with my melancholy, and me without Angela. Just what is it that drives us to do the things we do?

LATER...

My colleagues on this trip are a mixed bunch of souls, from all walks of life. Each with their own expectations, hopes and fears. And while I have rapidly gained the reputation of being "rather stand-offish", due to my need of thoughtfulness and journaling, I have made a friend in Michael, or Mike. Before the war he ran his father's farm in East Anglia, just outside Norwich. He is, as you may imagine, a tall, muscular man, as healthy as I am not, with a passion for all that is natural. He is also not totally sure as to why he is here, but firmly believes he is none-the-less, in the right place. He has two older brothers serving on the Western Front and felt it was his time to do something for his country, although unlike his brothers he has veered away from military service. I told him about my own previous experiences, which have served to underline his own beliefs in the taking of life.

LATER...

I wonder as I sit here in this isolated olive grove, looking out to sea and out to the immediate future, what I might add to the moving and strangely understated inscription attached to the larger of the two crosses on

Rupert Brooke's grave. I eventually decided, I'd add nothing.

And as I imagine them, distraught, probably weeping and trying to do their best in a situation that none of them had ever anticipated; I am filled with deep humility.

The scene falls into place quite naturally. The honours have been done, the chaplain had uttered the "Amen". The rifles have sounded across the valley, and with the main party departed, his five closest friends remain to put the finishing touches to the grave. They heap the marble rocks, so plentiful here, onto the simple coffin, and plant two crosses - one at his feet, and the other larger one with the inscription, at his head: All this done in moonlight.

As to the fate of those five, I am sadly unaware, which in a way is ironic. However, their dedication to a friend does them eternal credit. I see them clearly now, alternatively pacing around and sitting fretful by the grave; fingering the marble and clenching their fists. They are in a frightful state of shock, realising that things were in no way going to plan. They arrive as a party and were leaving with one short. The inscription records only what has happened and not what was felt. These men were numb with grief, but also with the nagging fear that Brooke wasn't after all immortal and now, what would fate have in store for them?

I am fortunate, by comparison. I come here to pick up the pieces of this failed military mission, not to begin it, as they did. Those friends may well be amongst those we bring back with us. Who can tell?

LATER...

Mike and I, dressed warm in duffle coat, hat, mittens and boots, lean over the side of the ship, under twenty miles from our destination. The day is clear, sunny and cold. He tells me these are the best days, the days that one has to keep moving in order to stay warm. My face is numb, my ears ache and eyes, through a screen of tears, search the horizon. When at last I catch my first glimpse of the Dardanelles I leave him to his perfect day and go back inside to warm up - as it may be my last chance for a while. Who knows what we'll meet there?

LATER...

Technically, the war here is not officially over, but it seems that way. From all reports, the evacuation has been, ironically, the most successful part of the operation. And similar to Brooke's burial, the majority of our work will take place at night, backed up with a squadron of destroyers, just in case.

We have been warned that the area, for approximately three to four miles around, reeks of death. And even on such a cold morning there is that suggestion, hanging there. They also say that early on in the fray the casualties were such that each side called a truce just to bury their dead! And it was not only due to the stench, but because of the hot Turkish sun that bloats and distorts the dead bodies so badly, that it was putting the British off the job at hand.

I am first amazed by how small the area of battle is. And then, with the scale in my head, the statistics take on a new meaning. Over 200,000 allied men were wounded and over 40,000 had died. "Where are they all?" I wondered, as I viewed the slopes and the hideous trenches through binoculars. Soon afterwards a colleague enlightens me, "Some of the trenches and the slopes *are* basically the dead". I cursed my naiveté.

As evacuation suggests, we have come here only for the living and wounded. They are all in a really terrible way. It's much worse than Ypres: as even the living appear dead. However, they are delighted to see us, and they clutch my sleeve and shake it, and look into my eyes attempting a smile, but all they can do is cry. It is impossible not to cry with them - they have been cannon fodder for months and it's a wonder that anyone has survived.

We pick up Canadians, British, some French, but mostly ANZACS, (Australian and New Zealand Army Corps), who also bore the heaviest casualties.

Disease is also rife, with all the decomposing bodies, which only serves to add insult to the already, momentous injury. At one point I was overcome with the sheer quantity of need. Everywhere I looked I saw hands reaching out accompanied by desperately sad faces that moaned and cried relentlessly.

You might, if you were either incredibly inventive or equally sadistic, imagine the wounds encountered there... I cannot, in respect of their hosts, describe them.

It took three days and nights to load the ship to its absolute limit, and by that third day the shock of the experience is beginning to wear off: Or am I still just numb? All we stretcher bearers are exhausted, emotionally and physically, and while our hearts bled for these men, there were still some I could not look squarely in the eye, so bad were their wounds. I've lost count of the times I was sick, from the sights and the smells.

It was Michael's first experience of such horrors and on the second morning he begged me to let him stay in bed, which of course I did. But he only followed on, ten minutes later.

LATER...

It was with immense relief that we 'set sail' for Britain. And while free time on this return journey is considerably less than our outward trip, I took a few minutes to watch, from the upper deck, the Dardanelles slip slowly out of sight and into darkness. It is easy to forget about the geography and natural beauty of a place under such circumstances, but with Michael as my guide, I was glad to see it for what it was. This was a ruggedly beautiful place, where in spring and early summer, he tells me, the whole landscape could burst into amazing colour and delightful aromas. This land too has lost its innocence. How long would it take to regain it and bloom fully once more? Michael assures me that nature is more resilient than human nature and next year the wild flowers and herbs would return, undaunted.

# JOURNAL: MARCH 11^(TH), 1916.

Today, a month or so after my discharge from active service in the Dardanelles, I returned to school for the first time in months. Spring is in the air and I wonder if it has also returned to Sulva Bay. Michael and I have exchanged letters, but I fear we have little in common now as we both have returned to our respective lives and share only the idiosyncrasy of a month at sea. And while the war continues its unbroken pattern, I am content to remain a bystander and await its end with acute anticipation. There is no more I can do.

Above all, I feel a deep-seated anti-climax. These past two years my life has changed so much from the one I thought I owned upon my re-entry into village life in 1912. And whilst the war has made such unexpected marks on all our lives I am forever the optimist when I say that war, like natural devastation, has its own unique value and meaning. I don't merely mean to justify war as some unavoidable entity that returns to us on a regular basis to keep us all in check, but there has to be more to it than meets the eye. After all, if there is a deep meaning, where might I ask is reason and purpose? I have given of myself and witnessed the greater sacrifices of my fellows, and now, two years on, nothing appears to have been gained. Am I too blind, or selfish perhaps for the real meaning to penetrate me? And so I am left, once more, with this emptiness where a sense of achievement might belong and I'm faced with a return to a pre-war life, with nothing resolved. It's futile, isn't it? It's the making of sacrifices without due return. Is it selfish to act without question and then complain that one is rewarded with emptiness devoid of any satisfaction?

# JOURNAL: NOVEMBER 12<sup>TH</sup>, 1918.

After my first experience of true anti-climax when I returned home from the Dardanelles in 1916, I wondered at the time how I would feel when the war was finally over. At the time however, I really thought the war would never actually end. Week after week, month after month, and year after year it dragged on, in colossal pits of minutes and seconds, marked only with despair. Despair, that became so much like a way of life, I for one thought the final hour would never arrive. Wars before now, so my history books tell me, lasted, with few exceptions, at most a month or so: This has lasted four years and three months.

And now it's over, it's hard to assess exactly how I feel. Yesterday, much to the displeasure of my neighbours and indeed, probably the whole village, I stayed in bed all day; sleeping, dreaming and occasionally reading. It seemed treasonable to even commit any thoughts I may have to my journal. And when I considered what the world had gone through it seemed unreal that yesterday was much like any other day. I don't know exactly what I expected, but it should have been more than just another day. The affront I felt at not being greeted with a sky of luminous rainbows - I'm afraid the average person would never understand. Tom and I talked. My parents called by and stayed for dinner. Tom and I, as always, shared philosophies, that back up Dr Manning's theory that talking is indeed the best cure. I will visit him again shortly when he returns to work in the new year: He's on extended leave at present, looking after his wife, and I hope himself, ever since the news came through that his son had been killed. They must have hoped Ernest would live through the war, but they hadn't banked on the German offensive on the Somme, designed to "beat the British back to Britain".

The statistics, for the record, are horrific to say the least.

Just before 5am on the morning of March 21$^{st}$, 1918; ironically one of those symbolically important days for me - being the first day of spring, when all might have been fresh, new and hopeful (I fool only myself). It was then that some 7,000 war machines sent about a million shells of various sizes against the British 5$^{th}$ Army sited between St Quentin and Peronne, in Central France. From the reports I've heard, the initial noise of the saturation barrage was described simply as, indescribable. An understatement might be "a sudden earth-shaking crash", or "an earthquake of unheard of magnitude", or even "a sound more terrible than Armageddon". One reporter wrote, "the earth seemed to twist and writhe beneath my feet!"

From all accounts the weather was suitably Shakespearean; cloaked in thick fog, accompanied by pouring rain.

The British knew that something was afoot, but weren't sure what. When that first terrifying crash thundered into their midst, they could only fear the worst. The barrage was followed by thousands of crack storm troopers who tore through the British ranks with practiced ease, aided by the weather, surprise and poison gas. All fortifications in the area - trenches, barbed wire and gun emplacements - disappeared into new craters, and men simply evaporated, with Ernest amongst their numbers.

Dr Manning said, when I visited him recently, that "it seems outrageous to me that a man can simply disappear. It's not as if we can, in time, visit a grave and pay our loving respects… but disappear, vanish… just like that…"

Ernest's demise is all too common, and one more

reason why I couldn't celebrate yesterday. There are families around the world, on both sides of this conflict, that are left with the uncertain knowledge of their loved one's eventual whereabouts. What can their hearts feel with nothing left to mourn but a handful of memories, some letters and a vacuum of emotion?

If I feel anything at all, it's relief. And while some folks' relief allows them to celebrate, mine won't. And now, to add insult to injury, I hear today that the influenza epidemic has returned to claim the unwitting in their misery and despair. The whole world's insane and even nature is against us!

Years from now, even when the survivors have been long dead, I vouch they will write books about this war and conclude that we were indeed all insane.

Today, I did at least emerge and go for a short walk. It was for me, a walk of remembrance. First to the open country where I could be alone with my thoughts and memories and later, after picking some wild roses, I laid some at the memorial for the boys, some more at Margaret's grave and the remainder at the foot of Angela's tree. I desperately need this world to be a better, kinder place, and in time it must doubtless improve. But today it was the saddest and emptiest of places. I want to die and leave it all behind…

# THE BURDEN OF GRIEF: CHRISTMAS, 1918.

Back at school, Howard's sadness was assuaged with his dedication to both English and handicrafts, together with the fact that the winter term, especially for the younger pupils, was always a time of the building excitement leading up to Christmas Day. On the last day of term the junior school performed the traditional nativity play, written, directed and tirelessly rehearsed by Howard Hardy, ably assisted by Flora Gardner. Flora, being the drama teacher, was responsible for producing two plays a year, and also for assisting Howard in the English department. It had also been Flora's job to resurrect the annual nativity play; a simple 25 minute version of the birth of Christ, that usually comprised of a dozen or so bashful youngsters, falling over, each other, their lines and their ill-fitting, slightly humorous, homemade costumes. Eight and nine year olds played shepherds complete with "horrible itchy beards" and "sandals too cold for any Derbyshire winter", whilst wise men had duly arrived, led by the light of a lantern, torturously manoeuvred across the back of the set by anyone tall enough to do so. Last year's highlight had not been, as was usual, the arrival of the Angel Gabriel, but rather the animated argument between Joseph and Mary as to who would hold the baby Jesus.

This year Howard, for reasons he didn't fully explain, had written some new lines and involved himself more in making "those 25 minutes more meaningful and engaging". Flora had jumped at this opportunity, as she had for the past few years been the one who gamely bore the brunt of the light-hearted, post-production leg pulling. Not that she minded of course, but the offer of help from Howard, she had seen as something close to a plea.

Rehearsals started at the beginning of December, with parents being asked to help prepare the costumes, with beards that wouldn't itch, too much. And for the first time in the history of nativity plays, possibly in the world, children were allowed to wear socks with their sandals!

Howard also encouraged the involvement of his handicraft classes to create a new set, using props that could be packed away neatly and used again in succeeding years. To create the maximum sense of reality both the star of Bethlehem, and the Angel Gabriel were to be suspended "with the utmost care", from a series of ropes, suspended from the ceiling. As she was both fair-haired and beautiful - and above all, the only one brave enough to fly - Emily, Tom's daughter and promising gymnast, got the job. There were those who claimed some kind of divine intervention, but, to top it all - as if it was in any way possible - Howard had argued that as they were a country school, "we should really have live animals in the stable". Flora had glibly replied that if they removed the roof they could also have real stars as well. But not to be put out, Howard reasoned that a few sheep (at least), could be penned just outside the side entrance to the assembly hall and let in for the brief show, without too much fuss. Further, if any of the sheep should need to answer "the call of nature, as animals invariably do during public appearances of any kind, a liberal use of straw could be depended upon to absorb the problem".

During the run up to the big night Flora became increasingly aware of Howard's mounting animation and agitation. And although she spoke to him as honestly as a friend and colleague could, he assured her that he was fine and was merely thrilled with anticipation for the nativity. Flora accepted this, but kept an eye on him and also spoke her concerns to Tom. For his part, Tom had already made mention of his own observations to Howard and had received much the same response as Flora. They would both have to wait and hope for the best.

As it happened, the play was a massive success, in spite of numerous calls of nature from the four-legged cast members. Emily, together with the slightly startled members of the audience, was so thrilled with her gravity defying performance that she took her final bow about twelve feet above the stage, with suitably angelic charm. What's more, beards didn't itch, costumes fitted perfectly and all had warm feet. A success indeed!

Afterwards, the buffet that Howard had planned at the rectory, was an equal success, culminating with staff and friends joining together to sing carols by candlelight, with Tom at the piano.

The poems of Christina Rossetti had long been amongst Howard's favourites and the highly charged "Remember Me", had become particularly so, with Angela's death. It was when the carollers began singing "In the Bleak Midwinter", also written by Rossetti, Howard's euphoria began to disintegrate. It was Flora who had noticed him slip away to the study, and that's where she found him, sobbing silently in the darkened room.

"Howard dear, is there anything I can do?" Flora whispered, poking her head around the door.

"Maybe you could leave me to it, Flora." Howard had snapped, startled that he'd been discovered.

"Okay Howard, just as you wish, but you know we all love you and care about you, don't you?"

Howard stood up and carefully moved through the darkness to the door.

"Flora, you are the dearest and most wonderful woman I know. What would I do without you?"

"Get a bit of privacy at least, I should think."

She was joking and they both smiled. Then she hugged him.

"Oh Flora, I loved her so very much... and I miss her terribly."

"I know, Howard, I know..."

# JOURNAL: JANUARY 7<sup>TH</sup>, 1919.

How hard it is to take stock of one's own position and situation. To effect thus, one needs the obvious facility to shed one's skin and become totally objective. There are always, or should be, three alternatives to offer the individual for a proper choice. In my case at present these are - What am I? How do others view me? What do I want to be? The overriding conclusion should answer the question, "Am I being true to myself? Samuel Taylor Coleridge had something to say on this matter:

> Alas! They had been friends in youth
> But whispering tongues can poison truth
> And constancy lives in realms above
> And life is thorny and youth is vain
> And to be wroth with one we love
> Doth work like madness in the brain.

I choose not to share at this time, what I gain from this, though I will say there lies a wisdom in these words that all men might do well to interpret on a personal level. What I will say is that rarely do the words love, truth and madness appear with such eloquence and reason.

I wrote this poem on the blackboard last term for one of my 6<sup>th</sup> form classes and left the topic open for discussion. It's fascinating what inferences and conclusions those young minds drew. I should add that I often present work that has a conscious bearing on my own life, a fact I feel able to share with my more advanced classes, with whom I have established, I believe, a quite mature relationship. I have also on my side a degree of, let's say, experience/adventure, that youngsters unfortunately see only as admirable, and where I believe it is my place to fill in those emotional blanks that complete the human picture: What use is experience without insight?

One young man, in response to my offer of open discussion made the following valid observation:

"Who is the writer talking about?"

To which I replied, "Who do you think the writer's talking about?"

"I think he's talking about himself."

"Can you be more specific, please?"

After some thought, young Robert Blight replied.

"I think he's falling out of love with himself."

For which he received some giggles from his friends. However...

"And what happens when you fall out of love with yourself, Robert?"

"I think Mr Coleridge means you go mad, sir."

Having someone else state only what you have, at best, only stabbed at in the dark, has an extraordinary effect on oneself. . Especially when that someone is a 16 year old, with an ear for poetry, but otherwise little worldly experience. Should truth be so transparent?

Thinking about "what do I want to be?", only reminds me that this path is closed to me at present. What of the future, when today is only a reflection of yesterday? It seems that life is standing still. Nothing changes, and everything is very, very familiar. Dr Manning once described it as "being stuck, somewhere between the past and the present". I have been seeing him again, on an irregular basis, as he has re-started his practice at Nottingham General.

I, of course, realise what he means by being stuck. Everywhere I look I see myself as being stuck. Stuck in the village, stuck at school, stuck with my life, stuck with my memories, stuck with my sadness... My God, the list is endless.

I remind myself that I am not yet thirty, but inside I feel absolutely ancient. I would still like to marry and have children. I still have literary ambitions also, as my poetry is something of me that I genuinely cherish. I presume if I were an ambitious man I would "strike out" and leave the village, join a new circle, begin again... However, I feel too broken, too weary, too angry, too sad, too fearful... Too lost. Life has turned into a wilderness that, I am ashamed to say, suits me very well at present.

I wonder *what* will become of me? Will I remain here, gradually collecting dust, as I allow the world to pass by? Or will I, at some point, stop the world in order to get back on? And what will it take for that to happen? If I send my poems to publishers for long enough, eventually something must happen, surely? Or perhaps a young lady will one day walk into the village and open my eyes to love again? Or more likely, I'll stay at the rectory with Tom, become the village eccentric and end up babysitting for Emily's eventual brood!

There is also mother and father. They will not last forever and someone needs to be about and ready to look after them.

I can't overlook my helplessness in all this either. It seems I have to tend the needs of all else before my needs are ever answered; although there is a safety in not identifying anything other than the basics... Oh dear...

What do I think, what have I become and what do the rest say?

In that there is a tangled web of lost chances. I can't or won't say I've made poor choices. I stand by all that I've done and consider my actions to have been honourable. Maybe it's just my response to certain key events that have let me down? Although I must say I believe that I have mostly, acquitted myself well. Is it just that some of us inevitably get the short straw most of the time, and are left trying to figure it out forever?

Actions, they say, speak louder than words, but I am truly at a loss as to how to act for the best. Better to be safe than sorry. And all this safety is eating me away!! I tell myself I'll know when the right opportunity presents itself, whatever it turns out to be, and yet with this blindfold of safety I wear, I wonder if I'll ever see it for what it is?

# DR MANNING: A MAJOR SESSION – JANUARY 12$^{TH}$, 1919.

Howard's sessions with Dr Manning, while beginning with a level of optimism had, by the latter end of 1915, faded out. Howard had never approached the subject of Angela as he said he would, choosing on the appointed day to revisit ground already covered. The Dardanelles trip that followed shortly after had, Howard believed, "served to lay the ghosts of 1915, pretty much to rest". All had appeared under control and Howard subsequently visited Dr Manning two or three times a year for what the doctor referred to as "obtaining a clean bill of health, for his peace of mind".

However, with the end of the war - a time that Howard acknowledged with a sense of relief - it became clear that this could only be a temporary respite…

After a frantic Christmas term, Howard had sought to use the school holidays to replenish his energies, yet all he seemed able to do was sink further into seclusion and depression. His immediate friends, alarmed at what they saw as a "return to the worst of the old days", cajoled Howard to visit Dr Manning before the spring term started on January 14$^{th}$, "just to be safe".

"What does it mean when someone confuses love for death?"

Howard had launched into asking one of many questions that he had been dwelling on now for more than two years.

"I think I may have an idea about the need for this question, Howard, but tell me more? It's been a while you know."

The two had briefly discussed Howard's friendship" with Angela, as he called it, at a session late in 1915.

Dr Manning had sensed concern, but Howard as always had been vague with his details.

"Whenever I think of Angela or feel love for her it's always accompanied by a sense of doom."

Manning accepted the use of the present tense, deciding to go along with it and see just exactly what was going on inside his client.

"Tell me Howard, does it feel as though you confuse the two feelings?"

"No. I'm afraid it isn't confusion. If only it was."

"Meaning?"

"Meaning... That when I see her I would prefer to think of finer things... Of romance, love , the future... Those sort of things, but I don't. In fact I think of quite the reverse."

"Is Angela aware of this?"

"No, I've never said anything."

"Do you think you should tell her?"

I'd like to, but I'd really prefer to understand it better myself before I burden her with it."

"Yes I think you're right. What else can you tell me about this feeling? Where do you think it comes from?"

"I was really rather hoping that you might help me out there."

"Really, Howard? Then let's go back a while, before Angela, before even the war. And if you had met Angela, or someone like her then, how do you think you might have felt?"

"I think I might have felt... young."

"And what does feeling young represent?"

"Oh I don't know... fresh maybe. Innocent. Not tired like I am now. Yes definitely innocent."

"And how do innocent young men feel when they are confronted with a beautiful young lady?"

"Terrified, I imagine! But seriously, maybe a little confused."

"So it could be confusion of sorts then? I think you're probably right, although terror does come into it at some time, I'm sure. In fact Howard, a whole army of feelings, attitudes and emotions rapidly rise to the surface. So maybe it would be fitting for us to consider more deeply what a loving relationship actually is, before we get entangled in those curiously opposing feelings. Is that all right with you?"

"I think that would be most helpful, thank you."

"This may take a little while, and as you're my last client for the day, I'll let this session continue to its natural conclusion. Is that okay with you Howard?"

"Perfectly so, Dr Manning."

"All right then. Now where shall we begin? Well, as this is such a broad arena for discussion, I'll endeavour to keep it to those elements that directly affect you at present, but forgive me if I either generalise too much or, through necessity, state the absolute obvious."

"No, no, that's fine doctor."

"Okay then. Let's start by dispensing with the obvious. I like to think, that in essence, the 'loving relationship', or LR, is the basis for all our human relationships. It's a blue-print, as it were. Much like the ten commandments that give us our moral grounding, although love itself is obviously not bereft of morals. And let's consider an LR as a general term that includes various forms of love like, motherly love, fatherly love, brotherly love, self-love, love of God and erotic love as its main components. Everything all right so far?"

Yes, fine thanks."

"Good. So if I can short-circuit this by presuming that you have experienced a healthy mother and father love that has inspired an equally healthy brotherly love and self-love, we may now discuss this subject close to the heart of every young man: erotic love."

"And if the previous loves have not been experienced in a healthy fashion?"

"Then that will become obvious along the way. You see Howard, It's a very natural process, a bit like mathematics, so should we get to a place where 2+2 does not equal 4, it will, I assure you, show up. Right, where was I? Oh yes, your reaction to meeting a potential girlfriend or mate. Let me substitute your word *frustration* with another word, if that's all right. Let's call that feeling, uncertainty."

"All right."

"Good. All of our feelings are connected in one way or another, but uncertainty, or perhaps doubt, would come before the feeling of frustration. Or, if you like, uncertainty can lead to frustration and is by virtue of this, a more primary feeling. Now, uncertainty is a feeling we all share, as certainty is all but absent in our lives. This might appear strange, but consider if you will the following. In life, the only sure-fire certainties are the past and the fact that one day we will die. All else are endless possibilities. And should you be thinking that you have any real, long lasting control over your life, consider this also. The main events in our lives - our birth and death - both occur against our will. Now, I haven't said all this merely to suggest we are all but helpless as to our destiny, but it does serve to illustrate facts pertaining to fundamental beliefs that should be adhered to in order to create a sound foundation for all future knowledge. Life is, after all, a continual search for an ever evolving and expanding truth."

"Absolutely doctor. Go on..."

"And so I suggest your feeling of uncertainty to be one shared by many, if not all, of the human race. The fact that makes your uncertainty unique is how it takes form and how you deal with it. And if we consider your reaction to uncertainty, as doom, how different would it have been prior to 1915? You see Howard, we have to acknowledge certain truths here. And the fact that you have sought my services after, and not before those events in 1915, leads me to presume that things happened during that year, that have changed your outlook on life. Would you agree with that?"

"Definitely doctor, yes."

"Hopefully, throughout this discussion today, which I hope is not too much like a talk, on my behalf - but that of course is somewhat unavoidable - we can start to establish certain facts and truths. And by doing this, help to direct you through, not only your problems with Angela, but also your overriding trauma that colours much in your life at present. And while one feeds and contributes to the other, at times their boundaries are difficult to define. So we must be vigilant in this respect."

"That's so true doctor, and something that I do find particularly hard to both separate and understand. Although I do see it as my attempt to do the right things for the right reasons."

"Good. Tell me more about that."

"Well, let's say I realise I can't take my anger, or whatever form it takes, out, indiscriminately, just because of what happened to me in Ypres."

"Which is a noble act, but as you suggest, it's hard to separate the 'now and then' elements. After all, we all get angry from time to time, don't we?"

"Yes, but I do try to direct it at the appropriate object, and above all, keep it in perspective."

"So Howard, what does an LR mean to you?"

"For me, I think I know how it feels or at least, should feel, but putting it into words…"

"You can be honest… Don't be afraid of making mistakes, there are no prizes."

"I know, I know, but I don't want to appear foolish."

"Just give me some words then."

"... Nurturing, kindness, devotion, hard work..."

"Yes, I think you're about on the right track. Basically, I think four words sum it up... care, responsibility, knowledge and respect. And in addition to these what act serves to embellish them?"

"Act? How do you mean?"

"Maybe environment is a better word. Or maybe, what can we do to encourage the LR?"

"Oh I see. Well, isn't that what caring is about?"

"Yes, I suppose it is. But GIVING was the word I was looking for. For as we give within this relationship, the whole world around us starts to give also; it's a curious dynamic."

"Yes, and I know couples like that, whole families in fact. Our family was much that way until..."

"Go on."

"You know...the war."

"You mean the war stopped your family from giving?"

"In a way it did... but you know what I mean."

"I know exactly what you mean, or at least I *think* I know what you mean, but it's your job to make sure that I know exactly what you mean. Yes?"

"Yes... yes. I'm sorry."

Manning rarely let Howard get away with generalisations.

"Don't be sorry, just be more precise. So what happened to the family then?"

"It got very difficult - still is really. It's as if love went out the window. They just seemed uneasy. And then there were the silences... deathly silences, where whatever was going on, simply dried up..."

"And what had changed to cause this?"

"It was as if they were angry with me... but I can't be sure why."

"But you must have an idea."

"...Well, mother said something about being scared to love me, but I didn't really want too many details."

"I think scared to love just about sums the situation up. You see Howard, true love, in any of its forms, must be without conditions. It is unconditional. It is also, and I use these words generally, without rules. But what you did, which is how they saw it, broke the conditions of their unconditional love for you. You broke the rules by becoming, in their view, unlovable."

"I think I understand. But do you really think that?"

"It's not what I think, Howard, is it?"

No... but it seems so cold. It's almost as if I arranged the whole thing - I did it on purpose just to shock them."

"And life is cold with them, isn't it?"

"Absolutely."

"You see Howard, we talk about unconditional love as if it really exists, when in truth, the best we can expect is a relationship based on varying degrees of conditions. Some of us are bound tightly and oppressed by them while others have much more freedom and movement. And a truly LR can only exist in freedom, with as few conditions as possible. What your family is saying is that they can't fully trust you at present. You literally frightened them to death, and that is born out with the deathly silences, as you call them."

"Oh my God... It's beginning to fall into place. It's as if they're treating me as if I had died, like I wasn't there anymore..."

"It seems that way, doesn't it."

"Do you mean they started grieving, even before they saw the body?"

"Now there's a question? Yes I suppose in a way

that could be true. Of course, they would have to join us to confirm it, wouldn't they?"

"Of course, but I don't think it's likely. Not just yet anyway."

"You see Howard, as I said earlier, this is your opportunity to acknowledge your own truths. Everything we need is here inside us, and other than my prompting and prodding, nobody else can help. We only have ourselves in these situations, with our own conclusions and truths. And coincidentally, both you and I work in environments that echo the LR perfectly. Student/teacher, doctor/client. There's a lot more to love than we think..."

"It's amazing what comes out in these sessions..."

"And we haven't finished by a long chalk, yet. So let's continue with the LR. In a way, an LR is much like the wedding vow. In sickness and in health, for richer and poorer etc. Because if there are no, or few, conditions, it means that everything that concerns the members of this process is fuel for the fire. So within all our relationships, we may talk about the good things and the bad, the happy and the sad, and nothing is unacceptable as everything is capable of enriching the relationship. This is true freedom Howard, and though it might seem far away today, practice, they say, makes perfect. And the more you give, the more you get back, and the trade, evolves naturally. So... let's consider Angela for a while, shall we?"

Manning had quite casually 'dropped' her into the conversation, hoping for a spark of recognition from Howard.

"Yes... I realise that I've only just met her, but I do have very strong feelings for her, and that says a lot for someone who never considered marriage to have a particularly, strong appeal."

"I think the appeal of marriage is based more on the

object of your affection rather than the institution of marriage, isn't it? I mean to say, a glass of water is merely that, until one becomes thirsty, if you get my drift?"

"I suppose you're right, but I must stress I never considered it would happen to me. All around me married life exists. After all, I am a product of it. But for some reason it has been something that lacked… what shall I say… definition, I suppose."

"I can appreciate that, Howard. I think most of us would echo those kind of sentiments, until of course, we met the right woman. And after all, let's remind ourselves that you have only just met, and talk of wedding bells, is a little premature at this time. Yes?"

"Well, yes and no."

"But isn't it human nature to go overboard in situations like this?"

"Possibly."

"Well, this is your first experience of this kind of feeling, isn't it? So Howard, other than terror and uncertainty, is there anything else you feel, that is relevant to your predicament?"

"No, I don't think so."

"Okay. Now you spoke earlier about how you might have felt if you'd have met your Angela character before your war experience, and you mentioned you might have felt young and innocent. And so now, in stark contrast, you feel decidedly uncertain, even to the point of doom - whatever form that might take. So might we deduce from all this that you have in some way lost your youthful innocence somewhere along the way?"

"By deduction possibly, but you make it sound awfully sterile, this loss of mine. Almost as if I went out one day for a walk and dropped it in the bushes, or something. That if I'd been more careful, I'd still have it today."

"Is that what you think, Howard? Have you been careless and lost your youth?

The mood in the room was changing. Manning could detect it, and he would now, as he suggested he might earlier, involve himself with some subtle pushing and prodding. Howard, for his part, had clearly gone on the defensive. He sat, legs crossed, arms tightly folded, slowly rocking in his chair, scratching his belly.

"My youth... my youth!!... I think I've lost a damned sight more than that, don't you? Bloody hell, what about home? What about school? I must have been incredibly careless to lose all that, don't you think?!"

Howard's voice quickly grew louder as his resolve wore away. And Manning, detecting that Angela had suddenly *left* the conversation inquired.

"And Angela, what about her?"

Howard continued to rock in his chair, but now his gaze was fixed. Anticipating what might happen next, Manning stood up and moved around the desk and stood beside Howard, with a hand on his shoulder. It was as if by this faintest of touch that Howard was awakened from a sleep. And slowly raising his gaze to Manning's eyes, he spoke, as tears of grief ran down his face.

"Angela? Yes, Angela. She's... dead, isn't she?"

"Yes she is, Howard. I'm most terribly sorry. And it seems the time is right for letting her go..."

# TOM'S JOURNAL: AN OVERVIEW OF 1915-1919.

It was a year that winter threatened to drag on forever with spring waiting patiently under the frozen earth to colour our lives, or maybe she had given up. At this time I became increasingly aware of a similar struggle going on within Howard. I saw it and it scared me.

With the memories of how he was when he returned from France still fresh in my mind; I recognised the alarm bells all too clearly.

But France wasn't the end of it for Howard. More an horrific genesis followed by two more crushing blows.

Directly after Christmas 1915, and in a matter of a few days Angela, one of the few anchors that kept Howard steady, was transformed from a healthy and beautiful young woman to a deathly white, barely breathing, corpse.

While the war continued across the channel with ever mounting fatalities, at home influenza took hold and killed with an equal lack of discrimination.

Howard had recovered sufficiently to return to school when the new term started in September. Thankfully, he was also taking the lion's share of time with Emily. For my part, Christmas saw me at last starting to come to terms with Margaret's death and my own self doubt as to my roles of father and minister. For a few days at Christmas life seemed more stable than it had been for months.

There wasn't a single area of our lives that hadn't been cursed by this war, and worst of all it had cursed our hope, forcing us to live tentatively and temporarily. No longer could we take tomorrow for granted, so we lived just for the day. We had become fearful of tomorrow and desperate to turn the clock back to a yesterday that once existed, prior to this curse. So fearful were we, that we tried not to tempt fate by throwing our hands up in despair and sighing, "things can't get any worse", when disaster struck, for we knew things had, and they got worse by the day. We were guarded and regularly held our breath, sometimes for days.

When Angela died I can only estimate how Howard felt. For myself, I was outraged. And while Howard fell silent, I did all the things I know I should have done when Margaret died: I was so very angry... I ranted and raved, I cried and screamed - and again my fragile faith was tested. I wanted to be like Howard, and be numb. But when she died I let out so much for all of us: Margaret, Angela, Emily, Howard and me. I was so deranged at the time I had no clear idea who I was mourning, and I wondered when it would end; if ever. And I saw at this time that it didn't matter. In fact nothing mattered other than me being able to feel..., feel something for someone, although regularly it was me I was feeling sorry for. Sorry for this sadness and sorry for not being able to show it before, for Margaret. But I learned through my own experiences and the testament of others, that in a world filled with so much sorrow, it is impossible to feel only sadness for one alone. This world is in universal anguish: It is inescapable.

I held a small, private service for Angela, and then her parents took her body for burial in Kent. This was something that Howard found hard to come to terms with, yet he bore it like some unavoidable snub. Part of the grieving process is to be able to visit the grave of the loved one. For him there would be no trace of her. She vanished as quickly as she had appeared. And a pale Howard was left wondering if she had ever existed at all. I tried to re-assure him with the universal grief our world was suffering, and how many fathers, mothers, sisters, brothers and lovers would ever visit or even find the resting place of their loved ones: The mass graves and disintegrated bodies of war.

Finally, he planted a tree in the cemetery saying, "there should be something left to remind us". The following week he went up to Nottingham and signed up for the war again. He answered the call this time as a conscientious objector, prepared only to save lives, not take them. The allies were in the process of evacuating their troops from the disastrous events in Gallipoli, and were desperate for stretcher bearers. Fate was with him - he left eight days later.

When he returned in April, a week after his birthday, he seemed much older. Although he wouldn't say anything about his time away, other than passing it off by saying, "there isn't much to describe about carrying bodies from point A to point B". Reading between the lines it was obvious that the experience had been a sort of blessing in disguise. A case of having one's mind taken off one disaster, by partaking in another, in the hope that maybe they would cancel each other out. Whether that happened, or if it was even possible, I don't know. Whether the pain was spat out or swallowed deeper, it was impossible to say. He said he wrote a journal while he was there, but burnt it on the voyage back.

For me, his absence was instrumental in forcing Emily and I together, just when it was needed. And it helped to direct some of that anonymous grief that spilled out for Angela, in the direction of Margaret. Emily and I shared so many tears that first week Howard was away: so great were the pent up and locked up feelings we both had. I even kept her from school for a few days, just to be close to her. And that closeness of her made the loss of Margaret less, as if there was something of her in Emily to nurture and love. I became "daddy" again, and we visited the grave together for the first time. And when Howard returned, he was still "uncle Howard", but no longer official guardian, and they have continued to be close. I know Howard was relieved I had finally owned up to my responsibility.

And so, that's how it's been since then. With Howard teaching. Emily growing. And me still doing God's work in my own unique way. Somehow life makes more sense now, and I am eternally grateful for that.

With the end of the war came a massive anti-climax. The prophecy I had made to Howard back in early 1915 appeared sadly to be true. And while crowds of people thronged and celebrated in the streets of London and other big cities, the general mood, besides obvious relief, was one of abject grief and what will be seen as, eternal regret. War memorials were erected all over the country in memory of those who had died, and in France and Belgium massive cemeteries are springing up to house the known and the unknown dead of all nations. Photographs in the newspapers show line after countless line of simple, white crosses , standing for the entire world like soldiers at attention, in a calm, endless sea of perfectly tended grass.

But the signing of a piece of paper on Armistice Day pays minimal service to those who suffered the horrors of war, or those left behind. Our village, as small as it is, still has a feeling of emptiness and loss. Wives without husbands, parents without sons, children without fathers. It seems that a whole generation has been sacrificed - and for what? A little bit of ground here and there? And I wonder what, of any real, lasting value, has been achieved by four years of endless slaughter. Our world has been dealt a blow no-one could easily have predicted. And with the obscene loss of life, both sides of this conflict have been united by the all too obvious fact that our lives, will never be the same again.

I re-iterate this recent past, attempting in some way to qualify the events of last week. Howard, like countless many others will live forever in the constant shadow of depression: A faceless and mysterious enemy that can worsen and strike at any time, without warning. In Howard's case of multiple trauma, his risk of breakdown is that much greater.

His edges have been well and truly warn down, and I know he feels he has nowhere to hide at present, such is his lack of reserve. If his mental wounds were made physical, he would be seen to be severely handicapped: this is my present understanding of his situation.

Gradually over the months he has opened up sufficiently to allow us to discuss, however superficially, his sense of loss. But I fear he will bear these losses and wear the invisible scars, indefinitely.

Early yesterday morning, just before six, I was woken by what sounded like somebody moving furniture about. On closer inspection I found the noise to be coming from Howard's room. If I didn't know any better I would have thought he was packing his belongings and moving out: Or maybe he couldn't sleep, and was doing some cleaning and sorting out, (or so I told myself). Whatever the reason, I decided to return to bed, but lay for a while listening, out of curiosity. Twenty minutes or so later I heard his door open, and then the stairs creaking. Again I supplied myself with an easy answer. He couldn't sleep so he's having an early breakfast, or he's going out on one of his walks. The sound from the backdoor hinges, long without oil, confirmed the latter.

Something made me get up and go to his room, only to find out what he'd been up to in making all the noise. I opened the door and looked in - it was spotlessly tidy. The bed was made, the drawers and wardrobe were empty. Four suitcases sat heavily by the door. His books were out of the shelves and stacked neatly against the wall. There were some pieces of paper folded on his pillow. I opened them and read the first poem... I began to sweat, but I didn't know why. And then, all of a sudden I did. I knew exactly what was happening...

I raced down the stairs, through the kitchen to the backdoor and out into the garden. I saw no-one, and didn't know what to do for the best. I decided not to call him, as one of us panicking was enough. There was no movement in the field at the bottom of the garden: where was he? The summerhouse, he must be in the summerhouse... I raced the thirty yards there and burst in through the door. What I was faced with left me open-mouthed and staring. There was Howard, sat at the table, where a tiny candle was burning, giving minimal light. I could make out that he had his face in his hands, and the revolver he said he never had, lay precariously balanced on his left thigh. As I burst in, he slowly looked across to me and sobbed, "I can't do it, Tom, I can't do it", and continued to sob loudly. I grabbed the gun and in a fit of rage ran out of the door and flung it way out into the blackness of the field. I returned to the summerhouse and threw my arms around him, cradling his head in my arms, as I spoke his name - time after time, after time, crying tears of sadness and rage.

# 1919

# POEMS ON THE PILLOW.

### 1

I now say I admired her
Now that I can't have her.
And that she was young
Too young
Too young and lost.
But not lost to me
Or to herself.
Lost to fate and hope
And a future
Out on her black horizon.

And now I say I wanted her,
But not like the moths
That bore wounds
In smart, new uniforms.
I wanted her as a collector
Buys a book.
To polish and dust
Her soft, pale cover
And to stand apart from her
Admiring the golden words
On her spine.

And now I say I miss her
Though time has damned the tears
I've shed. And now at times
I wonder where those few weeks
Fall into place
In a life so disjointed:

Snapped at the heart
And so willing to believe
It never happened.

And now I say I love her
In any way she'd let me.
Even me
With grass stains on my knees
As I crouch, desperately trying
To bring her to mind
Once more
As I do each week
When I feel that time
Has stopped still,
But I'm three years on.

And now I must say it's over:
Too late to climb again
Too scared to hope
Too mad to reason
Too tired to cry.

## 2

And three years on
Do your minds still stick
Like mine, frozen,
Forever young and hopeful.
Or has the flesh
Fallen from your bones
Exposed too long
To maggot and worm
Like well-cooked chicken?

But the wall says
We shall stay that way forever

Never growing old
To lose that fire and madness
That kept us sane
With once cool heads.

### 3

I know you are safe
Sad faces
With limbs torn painless
And eyes forever closed,
While mine stay open
Awaiting their turn.

My time, without glory
Or ceremony,
No manicured grass
No uniform cross
Just a trembling hand
In the darkness.

### 4

Paralyzed, I wait,
Not caring for life.
The thrill is gone.
No hope for love.
She too lies cold.

Not wanting salvation
I am alone:
Alone and eager to join you.

And why should it leave so soon?
Was spring so long
That summer never came?

I stand stiff with cold
Surprised by an early winter
That will crush all breath
From an unsuspecting life.

# JOURNAL: FEBRUARY 15$^{TH}$, 1922.

Given the benefit of hindsight, the twentieth century had begun, in a manner of 'almost too good to be true', for the population of our small islands, Great Britain.

The nineteenth century, I'm sure, had allowed us far more than we ever thought possible. And there are of course obvious problems associated with such Golden Ages, the least of which being its longevity.

And while I now see a sense of decline coinciding with the death of the main architect of that Golden Age, our Queen Victoria, in 1901, it would have taken a brave man to anticipate the horrors, lying just around the corner.

War has littered our history since time immemorial, but the Great War of 1914-1918 had something new to prove. Not only did it involve all the major countries of the world, it also robbed them of their finest and best, to the estimated joint losses of some twenty million men, women and children.

Today as I write this piece, the majority of which I am intending to send to the Nottingham Daily Record, I see a country so dispassionately unmoved by the events of 1914-1918, that I wonder if the sacrifice of so many, on both sides, was in any way worth it. I do realise however, that we did not go to war initially, to make improvements to our social standing, but the resultant of four years bloodshed should at least guarantee some fitting reward for the surviving combatants and to the sacrifice of the dead.

Today, some three years on from the peace of November 11$^{th}$, 1918, our land has been cluttered with fine memorials to the fallen: with bronze sculpture and marble tombs, the dead live on in our memories. And yet no-one has suggested why it happened. Was it worth the sacrifice, or indeed, what has been gained as a result. What is more evident is the inclination to deny that it ever actually occurred: a suggestion so ridiculous that it appears, on the surface anyway, to be a more palatable alternative for many.

And what do I say? I say it happened, by the simple virtue that I was present and took a minor part in it. And yet, why should the great majority prefer not to acknowledge its happening?

1) Grief. Pure and simple. Our nation is possessed with grieving and one of the initial reactions to grief is denial. And if we deny ourselves the acknowledgement of personal loss, how simple it is to believe that the war never happened. Also, I hear there are many widows who still expect their 'dead' husbands to walk back up the garden path and continue their lives as if nothing had happened in the intervening time.

2) Guilt. How could we, all of us, not feel guilty? The war has been won, but the overall cost has been cataclysmic. With forty percent of our young men dead, how can we feel anything other than guilt? And especially now when we consider the patent lack of reward for the sacrifice.

3) Shock. We are still, as a nation, in a state of shock due to the nature of our losses. I know people today who are still terrified by "the knock on the door, and the daily delivery of letters".

4) Anger. At both what has happened and what, as a result, is happening. Weren't we told that dying for our country was "proper and sweet"? How different the reality is with no husband, brother or son. With no provider.

5) We, the survivors. What are we left with? All of the above and much more. What of the loneliness, the sadness, the fear, the longing, the helplessness? The vain attempts at carrying on. After all we are only human, and when the above emotions do not find proper closure, do we not invert them in an effort to justify and qualify? For example, it is becoming more common to hear, especially among the parents of the dead, that it was indeed their fault that their sons died: That their freedom, through victory, was bought by their son's sacrifice. And in that, they would prefer to take the blame themselves, rather than to admit their sons had died for nothing.

And what does the government say or do? Very little, I'm afraid. Our Prime Minister, Lloyd George, promised to "build homes fit for heroes", but he has lied. In fact he has done more than merely lie, he has baldly turned and faced the past rather than acknowledging the country's grief, preferring to act as if nothing has happened. But much has happened. We, as a world, have lost much: our pride, integrity, decency, compassion; our deepest feelings have been cast aside. We have lost our innocence. Life will never be the same again!

What will it take for 'them' to admit it was all a terrible fiasco? Today the nation is still numb with shock and I feel that a plethora of well-intended war memorials, does nothing to placate the real underlying sadness of the "Lost Generation".

{Tom, let me know what you think of this. Howard.}

# JOURNAL: MAY 1936.

Sound in the knowledge that I will not, one way or another, live the year out, has come to me as an overriding relief, which in a way is surprising, as I was expecting to feel crippling amounts of guilt. In fact, guilt has become less a source of painful regret and more of an inevitable emotion, as say, a smile of happiness. If I could have my life over again I would only change one thing, and that is my serious nature: although I do actually regret very little, seriousness or not. It strikes me strange that we all question those so say, negative things in our lives, while simultaneously forgetting that we have lived much of our time with a smile, either on our faces, or in our hearts. Similarly I have sought to question much that has happened in my 46 years, yet strangely the inevitability of death I have not once sought to argue with. Is this death, or is this me speaking? I wonder? It comforts me to remember my parents when they too crossed the threshold I am presently negotiating. Their calm acceptance, and also I believe, a strong commitment to the hereafter. There were tears and sadness, with a reluctance to leave this earth and yet, both passed with smiles on their faces; smiles I believe they took with them to their lives beyond.

Enough of me...

Although relieved, I do seriously fear for Lois and Betty. Tom has promised that he will keep an eye on both and help when and where he can, but this doesn't placate Lois - and seriously, why should it? She and I have talked at length about what will happen *after*, but she still holds out for a last minute reprieve. She's angry with me and she's angry with God, and I don't see this fear of an uncertain future changing. While I, in this oddly serene and accepting mental state, can only beg her to have faith.

"Faith in what?" she says.

"Faith in life." I say.

"But life is cheating me by taking you."

"So think past your loss. What about Betty?"

"She terrifies me. How will I be able to manage alone?"

"You'll be fine. And anyway, there's always Tom. You know you can always rely on him."

"But Howard, you know it took me long enough to trust you…"

"I know, I know. But there's Betty now. Isn't she enough to keep you going?"

"I don't know, Howard. I really don't know."

And there are regular conversations on similar themes.

We have both agreed that Betty shouldn't know the truth. She can see that I am sick, but Lois doesn't want her to know about death and dying. I have to say I don't agree, but she can be very forceful at times, so I have so far complied with her wishes. I console myself with the belief that nine is not the perfect age to understand all this, which is very hard for me because I am very, very close to Betty: we have shared so much. If only…

And while Lois and I have had numerous talks on the subjects of love and trust I find myself all the while thinking of Betty who, if we hide the truth from her, may ultimately have issues during her own life, regarding unconditional love and trust.

# NOVEMBER 14<sup>TH</sup>, 1936.

Howard left their bed in the early hours of the morning and tiptoed to his daughter's room: she lay asleep and unaware. He knelt by the bed, his hands locked to pray, only inches from her face. He had rehearsed the words over and over in his head, but now, as he whispered them aloud for the first time, he was struck with terror. The palms of his hands started to sweat, his voice trembled, his knees were turning to jelly. His whole body screamed, "No!!", but he had to go through with it. Gradually he regained his composure.

"Dear God, let this innocent, sleeping child know the things that I have only distantly felt. Let her heart not be broken at my passing, though I fear it will. May her mother truly love her and may they both finally understand me, for what I am about to do. Most of all, Lord, let this child understand that I now walk the only path free to me... Let her know love, and in time, let her know her husband. Let her know her children, and encourage them to do what I have only dreamt of. Give her happy memories of me, that I may know I have been forgiven. Thank you, Lord. Amen."

Tears silently flooded down his face and he buried his head in the bedclothes and briefly sobbed into them. Then slowly he raised his head, half expecting her to be awake, but she slept on. He smiled and gently stroked her face and hair, and for a minute or so just knelt, gazing at her. Soon he would be gone and they would be parted. He would never see her grow up; to become a woman. He wondered again why all this was happening. Why he had been given so short a life; especially now when he had found such reason for his being? All this was beyond him. All this was madness, but unavoidable. He rose slowly and stiffly to his feet. His hands were now fists, clenching and re-clenching;

he wiped his nose with them. Through the curtains, he looked out through the window beside the bed and saw the stars shining. It was a clear autumn night. He would soon be out there, walking the hills and re-joining the land. Silently he dressed in the spare bedroom: all was planned. He went back, briefly into their bedroom and softly kissed Lois's cheek. In a way his illness had brought them closer, made them both more vulnerable, and he was glad. He whispered, "I'm sorry...", and quietly left. He took one last look at his sleeping daughter, kissed her again and smiled: he was doing the right thing, even though it was breaking his heart.

The last few days had been really hard. The disease was still eating him away; he felt wasted and spent. And all he had in front of him was a slow, painful death. He used the drugs he was given, just to be able to smile, think rationally, to make it through from morning till night: A life of lying around waiting for the inevitable. While re-reading Sons and Lovers he came upon the alternative, but there would be no willing accomplice for him, nor would he ask for one. He knew his wife and daughter were now dreading the long hours and days. At times there seemed nothing left to talk about, other than, "how long..." He loved them too much to expect them to continue this game of talking about everything... anything other than what was staring them in the face. They'd done their best, but the strain was plainly showing on their tired faces: would he still be alive in the morning? Would he wake once more in this world? Paul Morell had spared his mother's pain: Howard would now spare his own.

At first the idea repulsed him. "Kill myself?!" But soon he realised that that was all there was left for him to do. Once more he had a purpose.

Tuberculosis wasn't uncommon, and he'd seen others go the same way: winding down, gradually and painfully, slowly falling asleep. The drugs and the coughing. He's seen once proud men beaten to their knees, left without their pride, helpless and miserable. And the pain; that tight, inner ache, slowly but surely, twisting the last breath from a shrinking body.

For days he had wrestled with the idea until he had run out of the energy to think any more. The idea then became sweeter to him as he planned and re-planned his end. It was his life, his pain, his death. He had accepted the act and his acknowledgement set him free, "… until the end comes and I will be once more alone; alone but free."

That night they had played cards, laughed and chatted. Lois and Betty thought he showed signs of getting better, and they told him so, hoping to retain his positive spirit. He hadn't let on to them why, nor would he. At least they might remember him as being happy to the end - on the verge of recovery… anything other than a fading light.

They had all gone to bed in good spirits and he'd even managed to climb the stairs unaided. He wondered if he had the energy for the last walk into his valley. Downstairs he took three small letters from his jacket pocket and stood gently rubbing them between his thumb and forefinger. Three efforts of explanation as to what would shortly be discovered. He had tried to convey the truth regarding his decision, but resigned himself to the fact that they might only see the betrayal in his act: He imagined the three most important people in his life reading their letters and still asking "why?"

Carefully he placed them, side by side, on the kitchen table: Lois, Betty and Tom. He sat to ease on his walking boots, put his hat on, and then paused to look at himself in the mirror, one last time. He smiled and the eyes smiled back, while the face hung grey and gaunt. He looked away, half embarrassed, half in sadness and turning, opened the backdoor of the cottage, looked back just once and left.

Everything had been decided well in advance. He would go to his hill about three quarters of a mile away, where he would sit and administer his last *meal*. He imagined he would sit and gradually feel the mists take over his sight, his speech, his life. His arms and legs would become numb. Everything would centre in on his heart and lungs, and finally, they too would slowly give out. In his mind there was no violence, only a desire for peace: A need to shed the sick body and to go where souls go when they no longer possessed physical form.

He had often thought about heaven. What was it really going to be like? Who would he meet there? Would it be *heavenly*? He smiled as he thought these childish questions. What did it matter anyway, there was no real alternative. After all, he was healing what couldn't be healed here on earth.

He knew all this wouldn't go with him. So great was this burden that it had come between him and all he believed he was living for: His work, his wife, his daughter, his friends, his home, and his books... Again he cursed his luck, he cursed his lungs, and his blood. He stopped, and looking down fell to his knees and buried his face in the field's dewy embrace. His tears became one with the moisture as he cupped his hands to his face and gently massaged his skin. Looking up he saw the moon through the branches of a tree and the brightness seemed to comfort him.

Some two weeks previous when he had decided on his fate, he had felt not only a renewed closeness to nature, but also that a detectable surge of life had flowed back into his dying body. Not that he had boundless energy, no miracle had taken place: It was subtler than that. It was if his whole being knew that one day shortly there would not be a tomorrow. And as the allotted day got nearer his excitement grew to taste this new experience. Nevertheless, he was still losing weight, his breathing shallow and laboured, and his body a mass of aches and pains. But tonight all had changed. In kissing goodbye his earthly life, something deep inside had taken over, something so pure and unexpected that he had at first wondered if he had been miraculously cured. The *thing* he knew to be inside of him; his soul, spirit, his... reason, had appeared to have taken charge and now sat ageless and smiling at the very core of his existence. There was no longer pain and his breath came more easily.

He wondered at this dichotomy he was living in: The inside and the outside, the good and the bad, the sick and the well... the living and the dying. Only his eyes sat on the fence and saw all that happened, inside and out. How he wished he could tell his daughter and wife that he wasn't as sick as he thought... But all that was behind him now, and becoming distant.

He slowly got to his feet, and catching sight of his hill in the moonlight, continued on his way. Both his head and feet were light and he felt he was gliding through the long grass.

# LATER THAT NIGHT: NOVEMBER 14$^{TH}$, 1936

## MEMORIES OF WAR.

Howard's mind fell silent. He had reached *his* hill; that little mound of green he thought was his alone. His knees cracked as he gently sat down. "I'm falling apart", he thought, as he sat there and chuckled. He was on his own now, yet strangely, not lonely: He'd known worse times. After all, he'd been to hell and back, hadn't he?

But what was hell now? A distant memory? A thought that crossed his mind from time to time? A collection of images he saw in dreams? A look he saw on the face in the mirror? The sight of a man, no older than he, hobbling through town on crutches, with a leg missing? He'd been to hell and lived there for a while, but unlike many of his comrades, he'd returned. He'd come home. But with him he'd brought back bits of that hell; mangled, frightening images, that remained a part of him to the end.

There was nothing at all distant about hell. He had met it in Ypres and then renewed the acquaintance in Gallipoli. He could have easily avoided both meetings, but felt powerless to do so.

The experience was unavoidable. And he kept all of his appointments.

~ THE END ~

Lightning Source UK Ltd.
Milton Keynes UK
UKOW040640270213

206877UK00001B/9/P